TELEVISION TRAMP

TELEVISION TRAMP

EVANS MCKNIGHT

CUTTING EDGE

Previously re-published as *She Made Her Bed*

ISBN-13: 978-1-962896-00-9

Published by
Cutting Edge Books
PO Box 8212
Calabasas, CA 91372
www.cuttingedgebooks.com

CHAPTER ONE

A THROBBING pain, somewhere in the vicinity of the temples, relentlessly prodded him into consciousness. He tried, desperately, to woo sleep again but a dozen little devils with pitchforks wouldn't have it.

Groaning softly, Michael Carlyle opened his eyes and his gaze went automatically toward the table where the alarm clock should be. Then, abruptly, he was not the least bit interested in the time. A bottle flanked the clock. He let go a quick sigh of relief. It wasn't often he saved an eye-opener. It was odd, he thought. Even more odd was the plurality of glasses. One surely would have been sufficient. Still, the other might have been for a chaser—No. That wasn't right. The second glass had some obscure meaning; one which, for the moment, he couldn't quite grasp.

Painfully, he lifted his head from the pillow. He heard a sort of musical, gurgly sigh.

Somehow, he knew that this sound was connected with the presence of the bottle and the two glasses. But how? Cautiously, he moved his aching head in a horizontal arc. Eventually, he reflected without much interest, the riddle probably would be solved.

His glance was held by the chair near the window. Draped over it were sheer black nylons and silky pink things which certainly didn't belong in a bachelor's apartment. Yet, these things and the gurgly sigh seemed to bear some relationship to each other—and to the night before. Slowly, like the images in a telescope coming into focus, hazy memories began to take meaningful form.

He ran his tongue over his lips, hoping that his usually discerning eye for beauty had not failed him. Warily, he turned and looked at the other pillow.

Wide brown eyes met his.

"Sally!"

"You sound disappointed, Mike," the girl murmured in a husky-sweet voice.

"Don't be like that," he muttered, reaching for the bottle. He poured two drinks, handing one to the dark-haired girl.

"I really shouldn't, but—I will." She looked at him. "Thank heaven, I don't feel as awful as you look!"

He shuddered. "I must have gone overboard with the liquor. I didn't make an ass of myself, did I?"

"Except for propositioning every girl at the party and trying to get our host's wife to come home and spend the night with you, you were a perfect gentleman." Sally swallowed her drink and leaned back on the pillow. "It's a good thing old Conroy didn't hear you working out on Brenda."

"Well, as I remember—that gal wouldn't be hard to take."

"Beautiful, Mike. Radiant, in fact. But then, so's a big floral piece with 'Rest in Peace' on it. Of course, I understand that de Maupassant wrote that there's no sweeter death than to die at the hands of an outraged husband—"

Mike had gulped down his drink, had poured another which he began sipping. "I suppose today is Monday."

"All day." Sally nodded at the clock. "We're due at the studio at nine."

Mike put his glass down on the table. "We've plenty of time," he said, grinning. He drew closer to Sally, his fingers tangling in her dark, wavy hair. The hammering in his head seemed to have subsided. Maybe it was because of the whiskey. Or—maybe it was simply drowned out by the hammering of his heart as he looked down into Sally Kaye's warmly pale, lovely face. He felt her soft hands on his body. Her lips were parted in a secret sort of smile and her half-closed eyes glowed. The thought flashed through his mind: Sally has never been a disappointment during the year I've known her. Yet …

Why had he experienced that twinge of resentment when he had realized it was she who was at his side? It had been disappointment, all right. And, she had known it, too.

Why wasn't Sally enough? Whom did he expect to find in his bed, anyway? Helen of Troy? Just the same, he had to admit to himself that there had been the brief anticipation of—something different, someone new.

But why worry about it now? As his right arm went about her smooth, supple waist and his left hand cupped a velvet-smooth breast, sleep-sluggish blood came wildly awake and began rushing through his veins. His breathing became quick and shallow and, when he pressed his lips hard against hers, he wondered vaguely if any other woman could give him more than this.

By eleven o'clock, Mike Carlyle was aware that the pre-breakfast drinks weren't going to hold the little imps at bay much longer. He scowled at his typewriter and then at the dialogue he had written thus far. He wrinkled his nose. There was a mild stench, but it would get by—if it didn't get any worse. He stood up suddenly. Another drink was indicated. Something to anaesthetize pain—and memory. With every passing moment, the vague recollections of the night before grew a little clearer. What a damned fool he'd made of himself—

He flung open the door of his small office, strode along the corridor and, stepping outside, made for the bar across the street. Scotch over ice was fine medicine, he thought, making rings with his glass. He was beginning to feel considerably better. Looking up, he glanced at the mirror behind the bar. He grinned and the face in the mirror grinned back. It was a lean, olive-skinned face, high-cheekboned and—almost handsome. But all Mike Carlyle saw was that his thick brown hair was neatly combed, that his gray eyes seemed clear, that no one was apt to point him out as a dissipated old wreck of twenty-six.

Crunching chlorophyll tablets Mike returned to the studio where he was hailed by the girl at the reception desk:

"There's someone here for an audition, Mr. Carlyle—"

"Look, Hazel, you know I haven't the time to—" He broke off. From the corner of his eye, he had glimpsed a girl in a blue suit. She was coming toward him, smiling shyly.

"I—I am Eve Tremaine," she said with appealing unsureness.

Looking down at her from his full six feet, Mike felt suddenly and indomitably male. This girl was the very essence of femininity, from her halo of soft blonde curls to her tiny sandaled feet. Her perfectly curving figure was clearly defined by the snug-fitting suit. His glance lingered on her full, firm bosom.

Beautiful females were no rarity in the life of a program manager for a radio station yet, for some unaccountable reason, he felt curiously stirred. It wasn't that this girl was just another desirable female; it wasn't that type of attraction. He heard himself saying:

"I believe I can arrange to hear you, Miss Tremaine. That is, if I can locate our staff pianist."

"Oh, I can play my own accompaniment," she said, with little-girl eagerness.

"In that event—" Mike breathed deeply. He was imbibing the subtle spring-like fragrance which surrounded Eve Tremaine. "Follow me."

In his office, he smiled at her reassuringly and, picking up his desk phone, said, "Hello, Mac? Is 'B' free? Fine. I've an audition coming up. Heat it up and I'll be right in."

He led the girl into a studio where music stands, chairs, and several microphones in careless array were evidence of recent activity. He hung a microphone over the piano, saying:

"Keep the piano soft, Miss Tremaine. It's your voice we want to hear—"

When she looked up, he saw that her wide blue eyes had a frightened look.

He said, "There's nothing to be nervous about, Miss Tremaine. I'm going into the control room. When you see the red light come on over the studio door—begin singing."

In the control room which overlooked the studio, Mike said, "All set?"

"Oke." The lanky technician juggled snaky patchcords and flipped switches. The speaker over the desk hummed into life. He punched another button and the red light was on.

Her voice came in: *"I'm yours—"*

Mike straightened, watching her with a new interest.

The technician muttered, "That dame's got something besides a shape." He looked at his volume indicator. "She mikes like a million—"

Mike Carlyle nodded. Definitely, this girl had something. Here was a middle-register voice with a haunting catch in it. It had a living quality which the microphone caught truly. Her timing was good, too.

The song ended, but the tones kept resonating in Mike's consciousness. "Keep the studio hot, Mac—" Stepping from the control booth, he called out: "Try another, Miss Tremaine. Something in faster tempo."

When she had finished, Mike walked to her side.

"Now, I don't want to be too optimistic, but—you have style. I noticed it and the technician caught it too. It may reach the radio audience. If it does—"

Her eyes were shining. "Does this mean you're going to give me a chance?"

She was so charmingly eager, he thought. "How many songs have you?"

"Six or seven—good ones, I mean."

"Not enough. Still, we can use you on the *Thursday Night Frolics*. The numbers you did today, and—" He paused, nodding to himself. "I'll have the orchestra work up an arrangement. Be down at two o'clock Thursday for the rehearsal."

"I'm awfully grateful, Mr. Carlyle."

He walked with her to the elevator, reluctant to let her go. As he stood there, making small talk, he writhed inwardly. What the hell—she's a female, he told himself. If you want her, why not go after her? Ask her up to your apartment tonight; tell her you want to give her pointers on how to sell a song. Have the cocktail shaker out, and … It had worked before and it would work again.

But this girl was different. It wasn't only that she was so young. There was such an aura of innocence about her.

So, he let her go. Yet, the moment the elevator had whisked her from sight, he began regretting it. His mouth curved in a one-sided grin. Well, he'd got her telephone number. He would call her later. In the meantime, since a radio career meant so much to her, he would do what he could to promote it. He went down the corridor to Sally Kaye's office.

"Hi," Sally greeted him. "Better close the door—or is it just business that brings you here?"

"Strictly business, darling. A little job for the station's publicity gal. A new number for the *Thursday Frolics*. See if you can get a certain Eve Tremaine into the papers. She's new."

"I'll see what I can do. Get the lady to bring me in some pictures and interesting background material—if any."

They looked at each other appreciatively. When Mike had joined the small independent station a year ago, the ink had hardly been dry on his college diploma. It was Sally Kaye who had taught him to adapt his talents to the airwaves; who had instructed him as to the bewildering jargon and customs; who had given him all that—asking for nothing in return.

"Eve Tremaine—" Sally said, a bantering note in her voice. "Well, I hope this Eve doesn't feed you any wormy apples. Is she pretty?"

He glanced away. He didn't like Eve's name flipped around lightly.

CHAPTER TWO

I T WAS a bit after five when Mike ripped the final pages of his "Betty and Benny" script from the typewriter and stalked into Sally's office.

"The tripe's all cooked, darling," he said. "Suppose we dash across the street to Izzy's and surround a couple?"

"Don't look so grim, Mike. Every time you write one of those scripts you look as though you've been eating a razor-blade sandwich."

He sighed. "That pin-headed advertising agency! They insist that Betty and Benny sit on Hubbard Company furniture, drink out of Hubbard crockery, and cook on a Hubbard stove. Why in hell they have to gum up their entertainment—if that's what it's supposed to be—with a lot of stinking advertising—"

"That's what they pay you for."

Mike bared his teeth: "Benny, his voice trembling with passion, cries, 'Should I, or should I not—' And Betty, sobbing, says, 'I think you should. I really think you should buy Hotsox Hosiery, reinforced toes and heels at ninety-five cents a pair—'"

Sally giggled. "Just the same, Mike, you've made them cut down on the commercials a little—"

"Damned little."

Mike Carlyle had come out of college with printer's ink from a literary quarterly on his collar. As he'd told his fraternity brothers: "Radio needs some new blood. Right now, it's Coney Island in a fake mahogany box. But—"

He had not reckoned with the boys who pay the freight; with the gentlemen who bottle catsup, can soup, and sell automobiles...

Izzy's was a haven for the station staff. The smoky, shabby, little bar still looked like the hide-away speakeasy it had been thirty years before. It wasn't a particularly comfortable spot, but—Izzy was comfortable. He offered nepenthe in tall glasses along with good cheer in a mellow voice.

White teeth flashed in his dark, full face when Mike and Sally entered. He called out to his combination barman and cook: "Joe, two scotch in beer glasses for my frien's." Then: "An' how are all the radio programs today?"

"Foul," Mike said as he and Sally sat down on shaky wooden chairs next to a table mottled with cigarette burns and liquor stains. "Unspeakably foul, noisome, and—"

Sally said, "Harry Hazzard is just coming in—"

"Hell! It's bad enough having to be around him all day—"

The manager of the station was bearing down on them, a short, thin man in his early forties with sandy hair, crew-cut. Glancing down at Mike with his head over to one side, he looked like a defiant little rooster. Without waiting for an invitation, he sat down next to Sally. "How about you and Mike joining me for dinner? My wife is out playing bridge—At least, that's what she told me."

It was studio gossip that Hazzard and his wife were on the verge of divorce. Rumor had it that she had learned about the apartment which Harry kept for private purposes and intended to use this knowledge against him.

Sally said, "We'll have to make it some other time, Harry—"

The perpetual smile didn't leave Hazzard's lips, but his eyes narrowed. It was clear that he wanted company during the evening; a couple with whom to barge around the night spots until he found some female who wouldn't mind being picked up. "I don't see why ... " he began, an edgy note to his voice.

Sally interrupted quickly, "By the way, Mike has found a new singer—a girl—for the *Frolics.*"

"Have I heard her?" Harry asked.

"No, but you will," Mike said. "This girl's going places—"

"With you or me?"

Mike didn't smile. "She has an unusual voice. I told her to come in for the show this week. We can use her on the *Frolics* until she gets more experience."

"An unknown, eh?" Harry Hazzard moistened his pale lips. "The girl must be a knockout or else you wouldn't have taken the time to audition her. Well—I'll make a point of being around for the rehearsal—"

Mike knew that Hazzard already was thinking of the girl as a potential conquest. Mike dug his fingers deep into his palms, trying to restrain his sudden anger, wondering why he was so furious with Hazzard. Hadn't he done the same sort of thing himself, plenty of times? But Hazzard was such an indiscriminate bastard, a fellow who seemed to be driven only by the urge to reassure himself as to his manhood.

Forcing himself to keep his voice even, Mike said, "This Eve Tremaine is very unsophisticated—"

Hazzard laughed. "They all put on that act—if they think they can get by with it. Remember that little Parker dame?"

A mellifluous voice broke in: "Greetings. And how are all the dear little kiddies of radioland tonight?"

It was Hank Walton, the station's ad lib artist and master of ceremonies for the Woman's Newspaper of the Air show.

Walton put his arm about Sally. "Been true to papa?" Thanks to his donkeyish face and puckish manner, he could usually get by with things like that. But not with Sally, not when his hand started straying. She jerked free of his embrace.

Pretending he had not noticed the rebuff, Walton drew up a chair alongside Harry Hazzard. "Brother! Did I wow 'em at the Press Club with that one you told me about the farm-hand and the milking machine. Where you get 'em all beats me, Harry!"

Hazzard reached into his pocket and brought out a small notebook. "I heard a honey today. H'm—" He riffled through the pages. "Yeah, here it is—" He studied the cramped writing, then replaced the notebook. Leaning back, he launched into a tale about a recalcitrant zipper.

Sally closed her eyes. Maybe, Mike thought, she was trying to close her ears, too. It was a raw story, not at all funny.

But Walton roared, "Funniest damned thing I ever heard!"

Harry Hazzard beamed.

On the street, walking home, Mike took a deep breath of air. "That damned apple-polisher is after my job, Sally."

"Hank's out for anything he can get. But don't worry, Mike. Harry likes a court jester around yet surely he must know Hank hasn't brains enough to hold down your job."

"I wonder," Mike said softly.

He had a nice set-up, Mike told himself as he measured the vermouth into the martini pitcher. The apartment was compact, but the living room gave the effect of spaciousness. And, it didn't look like a furnished place. Probably, because of his few, but good, personal belongings: the spinet piano, the unusual prints, the books—

He poured a drink into a cocktail glass. He drank it down and nodded approval. Just right. Everything was—just right. The day had gone more smoothly than usual at the studio. Yesterday's hangover was a thing of the past.

The doorbell rang. His eyes went to the kitchen clock. Twenty minutes of eight—and he'd told Eve he would be expecting her at eight. But, maybe, because she was so eager—

He strode out to the hall and opened the door.

"Hi," Sally said. "Didn't have to run over to Oakland, after all. So, I thought—" Her voice faded. She was looking past him, her eyes narrowing. "Big doings tonight?"

"Guests," he said uncomfortably.

"Sure it's plural?" She gave him a quizzical look.

"Okay, it's singular. But, that's all that is singular about it. I saw Eve Tremaine today. She wants to get my reaction on a couple of new songs."

"Oh?" Sally had advanced a few steps, was appraising the living room. "Well, I suppose I'd better be on my way. Just the same, I wish I had one of those invisible cloaks. I'd get a kick out of sticking around, watching you work."

"Just what do you mean?"

"You're all set up for business, aren't you?"

He flushed, watching her glance veer from the spray of gardenias to the exotic print, and then fasten on the black dressing gown.

She picked up the silk robe. "Brother! A golden dragon embroidered on the back, yet. So, this is why I didn't see you at noon. You were out shopping for something that would slay little Tremaine—"

"Don't be absurd. I bought the thing for purposes of comfort, not seduction." He snatched the robe from her and walked to the hall closet. Tossing it inside, he turned. "I was just about to put it away when you arrived—"

"All right."

"And my old robe is shot. You know it."

Her lips twitched. "Feel silly, don't you?"

Damn it, he thought. He did feel silly. That way she looked at him—as though he were a sophomore. He said between clenched teeth, "Stop acting like a jealous female."

"I'm not jealous. I haven't the right to be."

"I'll say you haven't the right. You're not married to me—"

"I've gone along your way with my eyes wide open, Mike. Of course, I've hoped you would grow up. And maybe you will—" Anger edged her voice. "But I'm afraid it's going to take a long, long time and I seem to be running out of patience." She pushed past him and opened the door. "Goodbye, Mike." She glanced over her shoulder and their eyes met.

"All right, if that's the way you want it," he shouted. "Goodbye!"

The door closed behind her with a soft finality.

He stood there, feeling the anger draining out of him. "Sally—" he whispered. He couldn't let her go like this. There never had been anyone like Sally. Maybe, there never would be. He had to go after her, tell her how much she meant to him, tell her that no one else really mattered. Not even Eve.

He put his hand out to the door, then let it fall. Within moments, Eve would be with him. There was no repressing the tingling excitement that the very thought of her evoked. That delectable child-woman—so naive and yet so voluptuous. It seemed that every detail of her being was acid-etched in his memory.

Still, when she came into his living room, he realized that the picture he had carried of her in his mind had been hardly more than a sketch. He hadn't remembered how her eyes had shone, glowing with innocence and—with amorous promise. Or that the demure smile was formed by such sensuous lips.

His hands weren't too steady as he helped her take off her coat. Then, when he looked down at the simple gray dinner dress with its plunging neckline, he caught his breath. Fascinated, he stared at the curve of that full, virginal bosom. With a perceptible effort, he drew back from her. He'd thought himself civilized, yet it took every ounce of his will-power to keep from crushing her to him, heedless of her desires. Until this moment, he had never been able to understand the urge to ravish.

She must have seen the look in his eyes, but it was as though she didn't understand. Tilting her glistening, golden head, she glanced about blithely. "This is a charming place, Mr. Carlyle." Like a bit of floss silk, she floated toward the piano.

"Just a minute, Eve—" If his voice sounded strained and unnatural, she didn't seem to notice it. "I've cocktails on ice."

"Later, maybe. But right now I do so want you to hear these songs I have been working on. May I?" She edged toward the piano bench.

He nodded, not trusting himself to speak. Perhaps, he reflected, it would be better this way. In a little while, he would have himself under control, would be able to use his head. And he'd have to. A girl like this one would require considerable finesse.

He sank down in a chair and, closing his eyes, listened as she sang. When, finally, she was through, she turned from the piano and looked at him with hopeful inquiry in her artless eyes. "Was that all right?"

"Much better than all right," he said sincerely. "You're good, Eve. And if you're willing to work, and if you have the time—"

"I have. Particularly for the next six months. My Aunt Agatha left for Europe and so I won't have to tag along with her on her social rounds."

Mike raised his eyebrows. "Mean to say you're Agatha Tremaine's niece?"

"Why, yes. I thought you knew."

"I didn't." He wrinkled his forehead. "I don't get it, Eve. With one of the richest women in San Francisco for an aunt, you shouldn't have to worry about earning a living—"

"But don't you see, I want to be more than just Agatha Tremaine's niece. I want to be a somebody. And"—she clasped her hands tightly and leaned toward him, "—and I will!"

For the first time, he perceived the aggressive angle of her jaw and, for an instant, he though he saw an inherent hardness.

Yet, the moment she straightened, he told himself he'd been mistaken, that it had been merely the way the lamp light had fallen on her face.

Now, she was smiling, was walking over to the record player, was choosing a record. "I'd like to dance, Mike. Would you?"

He went to her side and took her into his arms. Gently, at first. But then, suddenly, his embrace tightened. Every vestige of self-control left him. With one arm, he held her tightly as his avid fingers played over her flesh.

"No!" she cried, struggling futilely.

He didn't hear her. He had lifted her in his arms, had carried her to the couch and now her cries were muffled by his bruising lips. His hands slid along the warm flesh of her thighs and then, with a kind of savagery, clawed at lacy nylon.

He rose up slightly and before his burning mouth closed over hers again, she sobbed, "Mike, don't. Please—I never—"

A moment later, her words had meaning for him. With a strangled moan, he released her and staggered to his feet. She lay there, her head buried in her arms, sobbing brokenly.

"I'm sorry, Eve," he said hoarsely.

She looked up at him, her eyes bright with tears. "I know there's a price to be paid for a career, but—I just couldn't go through with it—"

"Stop it, Eve. I'm not expecting anything like that."

"Do you mean you'll still give me a chance, even if I—"

"Of course," he said gently. "And now, I'm going to take you home."

Home was a mansion on Washington Street. He walked with her through a sunken garden to an impressive, porticoed entrance. He did not try to kiss her goodbye, to touch her. He knew he was acting silly, knew he sounded like a high-school kid on his first date—but he couldn't help it.

It was such an amazing thing, this subtle blending of tenderness and passion. Could it be that this was—love? He wondered about it as he drove back downtown. Love—and marriage to follow? His fingers tightened on the steering wheel. Marriage wasn't for him. He knew too much about it, had seen what it did to other men. Tied them down and kept them from taking the long chances which a man has to take in order to be a success.

He glanced at the dashboard clock. Just a little after nine. Too early to go home—feeling the way he did. A drink at Izzy's and, well, maybe Sally would be there. If she weren't, he'd call her up—

She was at Izzy's. Her lips trembled as he came toward her.

"Still angry at me, Sally?"

"Oh, Mike. You were right. I was just plain jealous."

"You didn't really mean it when you made with that bitchy goodbye?"

"No." It was a muted but eloquent sound.

"Let's get out of here, Sally. Waiting for us at my place is some of the best gin ever to leave London. What I want right now is a jug of Martinis, and thou—"

"Mike," she breathed, looking up at him.

He saw the bright ardor in her wide, dark eyes. It aroused him to an eagerness that made his voice shake as he whispered, "Sally, you're a doll. A living, breathing doll."

Leaving Izzy's, they made a quick trip of it to Mike's place. Once upstairs and inside the apartment, they fell into each other's arms.

"Oh, you doll. You lovely doll."

"Mike, shut up and kiss me."

Lips met. Limbs met. He carried her into the bedroom, and flesh met.

CHAPTER THREE

S ALLY KAYE typed out the words: *For release June thirteenth.* That would be the day after tomorrow.

The thirteenth—unlucky day, she mused dully. It had been on the thirteenth of May that Eve Tremaine had walked into the studios for the first time.

Looking back, Sally knew she had sensed the change in Mike's attitude almost from the beginning. Eve hadn't been just another girl to Mike Carlyle, someone to pursue briefly and discard hastily.

Was it possible, she wondered, that Mike was in love with the girl? She bit her lip. Mike and she had always scoffed at "love." They had looked disdainfully at the young fools who mistook biology for romance and rushed into marriage. She remembered how Mike had nodded agreement when she had once said:

"It was sound—that old Tahitian custom. Young people experimented until they found the one perfect mate."

"And have you experimented?" Mike had asked.

She had looked at him candidly and told him about the young artist from Laguna Beach. Then she had added, "That's been over for a long time. I haven't been interested in anyone else." Her eyes had not wavered. "I think, though, I could be interested in you."

And that had been the start of it. For months, now, she had realized that Mike was the one for her. They looked at the world from the same vantage point, experiencing mutual delight in each other's minds and bodies. It was almost a perfect relationship and she was confident that it could endure.

But during the past weeks, night after night had been merging into the wake of time. Mike was spending fewer and fewer hours with her. He told her there were scripts to work on, new ideas to develop, but Sally knew better. She knew he was with Eve Tremaine.

Why couldn't he see the girl for what she was? A spoiled, selfish brat...

Well, it was no good thinking about it. With a sigh, she went back to typing the publicity releases. When she finished, she thrust them into envelopes addressed to the radio and TV editors of the Bay Region newspapers.

Mike had left the station a half hour ago. She'd seen him stride by her office. He had not looked her way.

"Oh, Mike. I love you so—"

Look, baby—there are lovers, and people who make love but, as for the word love—

I know what you mean, Mike. Love-stuff, that syrup sold for gold by songsmiths, story-writers, and politicians. Synthetic. Fashioned by morons for morons, guaranteed to blot out reality—

That's right, baby. Listen to the spieler: Step right up, ladies and gents, get your bottle of sentimentality. With every fifty-cent bottle, you get absolutely free, a pair of rose-colored glasses. Turn your blues into pink sunshine. Better than opium...

"Hallo, Sally," Izzy greeted her. "Where's Mike?"

"He told me he was working tonight."

"That boy. He work too hard. He don't come to see me no more. What you want, Sally?"

"Scotch—in a beer glass, Izzy."

As Izzy turned away, Sally felt an arm slipping about her shoulders. She looked up at Hank Walton, and said with annoyance: "Go away, Hank. I'm in no mood for a master of ceremonies."

"Out to drown your sorrows, eh?"

Hank was on the scent. Sally saw it in his watery blue eyes. His long nose could sniff out a dying romance and, like a vulture, he moved in fast, hoping for a feast. He didn't get his teeth into anything very often, but it wasn't for lack of trying.

Smirking over the rim of his glass, Hank said, "I've got the keys to Harry's apartment. How's about some brandy and champagne—"

A creamy voice cut through the smoke and the cacophony of voices: "Hello, Sally—"

"Mary!" Hank exclaimed enthusiastically. "Come over here to daddy."

Mary Sweet joined them, a tall shapely girl possessed of a lilting, velvety voice which made radio listeners think of glowing fireplaces and cradles. Mary seemed to be able to make any song sound like an exalted lullaby.

She ordered a sherry and, turning to Sally, said, "Thanks for the grand write-up the other day. It was a swell job and I do appreciate it."

Sally smiled. "Have to keep our stars shining." She paused. "Mary—is anything wrong? You look like you've lost your best friend."

"You can say that again," Mary murmured. "My nice lieutenant shoved off tonight. Orders. You'd think there was a war on, or something."

Sally saw Hank Walton's nostrils quiver. Damn him, anyway, she thought. He's going to move in and...She shrugged. Well he'd been waiting for his chance at Mary a long time. As for Mary—she'd been in bed with practically every other male at the station. So why not with Hank?

It wasn't that Mary was really a nymphomaniac, Sally reflected. It was just that Mary wanted men to be nice to her and she had long since found out that men expect certain considerations in return for being solicitous escorts. And, as Mary said, why fight with them about something you enjoyed so much yourself? True, there were a number of wives who wouldn't speak to Mary. But on the whole, Mary Sweet was considered very entertaining.

Hank's arm was about Mary's waist. "How's about hitting a few high spots, keed? And, afterward—"

Sally watched them leave. Mary would be finding consolation. Why not take a leaf from Mary's book?

After all, Mike had made no effort to get together with Sally since that big night those weeks before. And he didn't bother to come to Izzy's any more. So what was the use of constantly waiting around in the hope that sooner or later he would drop in for a drink or a meal and she would be able to see him, talk to him? Better to do as Mary did.

Sally put down her drink and, murmuring a goodbye to Izzy, started for the door. She would forget Mike from this night on. She would find someone else, maybe one of those older fellows, wealthy and suave. Or even someone like—well, someone tall, lean-faced, with eyes that twinkled with humor one moment and glinted dangerously the next—like ....

No.

Oh, Mike! Maybe if you held me in your arms once more.

It was past six, but the summer sun was still riding high. She walked aimlessly, not wanting to return to the stuffy rooms in which she lived. She was not actually intending to go near Mike's apartment.

Yet she was quickly drawn there by some inner compulsion. She looked at the building across the street. Perhaps, if she saw him—She was about to step down from the curb when she saw his convertible come around the corner. Eve Tremaine was with him.

They got out, laughing, loaded down with delicatessen packages. So, Eve was to play at being the little housewife—

Sally thought of the dinners she had cooked at Mike's. There had been that time the pork chops burned to a crisp— "Seared by our passion, no doubt," Mike had said.

Sally saw Eve reaching into his left pocket. For his keys—

She remembered those times she had fumbled for his keys, had opened the door, had rung for the elevator—Her eyes filling with tears, she turned away.

The next morning, Mike stopped by Sally's office. "You wanted to see me?" he asked.

"Yes. I thought I'd better let you know. Harry Hazzard's found out that Tremaine's fan mail is on the increase. You know what that means, of course—"

"He'll want to shove her into every dinky, stinky show we've got—making hay while the sun shines." Mike swore under his breath. "Thanks to Hazzard, there've been a lot of promising youngsters who've never got the big break because all the cheap shows they've been in make potential sponsors think they must be bargain counter singers."

"I won't argue with that."

"I'm glad you told me, Sally. I'll have a talk with Eve, explain to her what she's up against and advise her on how to handle Harry—"

"She might not want to listen, Mike. Ambitious girls are sometimes very impatient."

Sally Kaye was right. A potential sponsor heard Eve and wanted her. His name was Tibbs and he was a mattress manufacturer.

He came into the station the following morning, shopping for a radio program. The sales manager called Mike in and said:

"Mr. Tibbs would like to meet Eve Tremaine. Will you take him over to Studio B, Mike?"

Mike nodded and looked at the mattress magnate. There was something repugnant about the man; it wasn't only the fat, doughy cheeks and the thick coarse lips. It seemed to Mike that there was an odor of decay emanating from Tibbs, an odor that was accentuated rather than concealed by a liberal dousing of cologne.

"I want to see what this dame looks like before I sign anything—"

"What's the difference? I thought you were interested in a radio deal—not televison."

Tibbs grunted. "I don't buy nothing without seeing it with my own eyes."

With the office of the sales manager well behind him, Mike said, "To be frank, we've been saving Miss Tremaine for something good."

"Ain't my program good? Ain't my money good?" the mattress-maker exploded.

"What I meant was—with Miss Tremaine you'd have to have an orchestra. And I wasn't sure you'd care to spend that much money."

"She don't need a big orchestra, does she? Why can't she just have a piano?"

Harry Hazzard came up behind them. "I overheard what you said, Mr. Tibbs. An excellent ideal Don't you think so, Mike?" Hazzard was hoping to sign up the manufacturer in a hurry—and without an audition. Auditions meant extra pay for the union musicians. "Come into my office, and—"

"I want to give this dame the once-over, first."

Harry Hazzard took the man's arm, led him into Studio B. "Well?"

Eve Tremaine was not on the air at the moment, but she was going through her paces with the aid of Max Ralley, the staff pianist and a quite clever musical arranger. Max, his eyes closed, was listening painstakingly to Eve's delivery of a popular ballad, while his fingers thumped out stop-chords in open harmony. At the end of each phrase he inserted a figure in the bass. This "hat arrangement," as the musicians would call his improvisations, took some of the banality out the piece and added musical values, while at the same time Eve chanted huskily and with beautiful control.

Mr. Tibbs, however, was not listening. He was looking. The sight of Eve, in person, apparently was enough to overwhelm him. His knees shook a little. He panted. Beads of perspiration broke out on his flushed brow as he stared avidly at the girl's long, silky legs. His eyes popped at the sight of her curving hips, her breasts rising and falling as she breathed the song's phrasings.

Tibbs ran his tongue over his thick lips. "I'm buying," he muttered. "You work out a nice theme song for me. And put in some stuff about how Miss Tremaine keeps her voice in such top condition by having a comfortable sleep on a Tibbs mattress every night."

Mike winced.

"Sure thing," Hazzard said emphatically. "We'll work it out, all right."

"Another thing," Tibbs said. "I want to meet the little lady."

Hazzard promptly interrupted the rehearsal, and the introductions were quickly made. When Eve gathered that Tibbs wanted to sponsor her, she quit looking at him as if he were some species of dead fish. In fact, she became all coos and smiles. He beamed, managed to touch her a couple of times with fluttering paws. Max tactfully remembered that he was due in another studio, walked out with Hazzard close behind him. In disgust, Mike followed them into the hallway.

Later, much later, over sandwiches and beer, Mike said, "He asked you out with him, didn't he?"

"He wants me to have dinner with him tonight."

"Oh, he does, does he?"

"Well, what's wrong with that, Mike?"

"Nothing, maybe. Just the same, young lady, you're not going to have dinner with him tonight, or any other night."

"Why not? I have to be nice to him, don't I? I do so want a sponsored show, Mike. Do you blame me?"

He could not be angry with her, not when she was sitting across from him with such a wistful little smile on her lovely, innocent lips. He said quietly, "His would be a cheap show, Eve. The first of many cheap shows you'd be sucked into, once you started. You'd find yourself in the two-bit circuit forever—labeled for life, understand? Now, listen to me...."

He went on talking, and he saw after a while that she was beginning to be convinced by his arguments. She put her elbow on the table, rested her chin against the back of her hand, listened with wide-eyed attention.

"Then you think, Mike, that I should hold out for something bigger and better, is that it? If I don't settle for less, maybe one of the networks will pick me up and—"

"Exactly. Locally you're making a bit of a stir already. It's just a matter of time before the top bananas notice you...And don't forget, with your looks you're a natural for television. Hazzard will try to finagle you into taking this singing chore for Tibbs, but you can refuse."

"Oh, Mike." The blues eyes became tearful. "I've done a terrible thing. I've already signed up!"

She was so pathetic and appealing in her distress, like a little girl who had lost her candy. He smiled gently.

"I can find an out for you, Eve."

"How, Mike? What can I do?"

"Look, Tibbs hasn't signed anything yet. I know that for a fact, because he would want to take you out and—uh—sample your wares."

"So?"

"So just break your date with him tonight, and he won't sign at all."

"It's as simple as that?"

"It's as simple as that," Mike said.

Everybody at the station was talking about it. "Mike's done wonders with Tremaine—"

In less than a month, all traces of Eve's original nervousness had vanished and now even not too senstive ears could recognize the unusual tonal quality of her voice.

Mike had coached Eve in microphone technique, pointing out the advantages of stepping back a pace or turning the head sidewise during a crescendo; and how to caress the mike on the softer passages.

"Think when you sing, Eve. Think of the people who are listening."

Together they sat on the piano bench, Mike tense and straight. His longing for her had not lessened but that wild urge to possess her was held in check by an even stronger emotion—a desire to protect her from the world and himself.

A month before, and he would have laughed at anyone who predicted he'd be thinking of marriage before he was thirty-five or forty. He'd have argued that only a fool ties himself down and gives a hostage to fortune, and that he wasn't a fool. But now, he was seeing things differently. He was wondering if marriage might not provide him with needed stability, might not enable him to concentrate on his future, might not give him something to work for.

It was time he started moving up. He had served his apprenticeship in the coffee-grinder. He was ready to climb into the big league, into television. He would take Eve with him—right up to the top.

He suddenly became aware that he was not alone.

Sally had entered and was standing by his desk. "If I may interrupt," she said, "I must admit that Tremaine is a find, all right. The radio editors are beginning to take her up. Some of these items"—she flung a sheaf of newspaper clippings on Mike's desk—"did not come out of my office. Columnists are dreaming up their own stuff about her."

"That's a switch," Mike admitted.

With an interest he did not have to simulate, he pored over the clippings. Even when he had finished with them, he did not lift his head. He could not get himself to meet Sally's eyes.

"Thanks for bringing them in," he said. It was a polite dismissal.

Mike did look up from his typewriter with enthusiasm when, ten minutes later, Ted O'Neill walked in. Ted was the radio and television editor of the *Evening Record*.

"Hey, Ted!" chortled Mike. "Where the hell have you been keeping yourself?"

"Been keeping myself busy." Ted O'Neill tossed his hat on Mike's desk, smoothed back his crisp auburn hair, and then settled his stocky figure in a chair. "Having finally observed that radio-television editors rarely get paid what they're worth, I've been seeking other ways of carving out a future for myself."

"You never were what I'd call handy with a chisel."

A slight smile played over O'Neill's freckled face. "Chisels aren't necessary, boy. There are more ways to skin a cat than with a chisel. Look, boy—can you take time off for a quickie?"

"Can I!" Mike was on his feet. "I've been dreaming about a drink."

They were close friends, these two; had been ever since Mike's first days in broadcasting. Mike didn't remember it, now, but it was Sally Kaye who had introduced him to Ted. "I think you'll like him, Mike. He's sound—"

It had been good knowing Ted O'Neill. He was solid but not stuffy, had a level head on his shoulders and a rare sense of humor. Walking across the street to the bar with him, Mike thought: I've known other guys longer, but this guy is the best friend I've ever had.

They sat in a booth and ordered highballs. Mike said, "Do you know it's been more than a month since I've seen you?"

"I've been in Hollywood, boy." Ted grinned. "Writing a column is a nice soft job, particularly when there's a gal like Sally Kaye sending in stuff you can let run as is. But like everybody else, I've got the itch for dough. Must be contagious. So, I'm going to stick around where the money is—which means Hollywood and television."

He was back in town only long enough to clear up a few loose ends and then he would clear out for good, he told Mike. "By the way, that Eve Tremaine seems to be coming along right well. Where did you get her?"

"Dropped in for an audition, one day. Straight from heaven. What do you think of her?"

"Unusual voice. Natural stylist. Likely to go places. I was talking with Terris, down at Continental, the other day. He's been listening to her."

"What did he say?"

"Terris didn't tip his hand, but I wouldn't be surprised if he started making offers." He looked at Mike thoughtfully. "The idea doesn't appeal to you, does it?"

"Not one bit. She's network material, but I intend to see her go up the right way. Y'know, Ted, if it weren't for me, she wouldn't be in this racket. It's up to me to look out for her. She's so damned young."

"And damned good-looking, judging by the publicity photos. But she isn't in Sally Kaye's league—she hasn't Sally's class. Watch your step with Tremaine, boy."

Mike bridled. "What are you getting at?"

"Look, I'm just trying to make like a pal. Don't do anything hasty, no hasty decisions, boy."

It's not a hasty decision, Mike assured himself after Ted had gone. It's something I've been thinking about consciously and subconsciously for weeks. I can see how it is, now. I need her. She needs me. She'd be completely lost without me...

CHAPTER FOUR

MIKE PARKED his car atop Telegraph Hill, high above a bay which had been transformed into molten gold by a yellow moon. "Eve?"

She looked at him from under her long lashes, recalling what the girl at the station's reception desk had said that Monday morning, weeks ago. "Well." Hazel's glance had swept over her. "I guess Carlyle will give you an audition. But I'm warning you, kiddo—he'll get ideas. And like every other gal, you'll probably get ideas of your own. But it won't do you any good. Mike Carlyle isn't the marrying kind ... "

Eve felt a triumphant little glow, sitting there beside Mike in his car. Within moments, he would be asking her to marry him. She was very confident. Intuitively, she knew that the opposing forces inside him had battled to a finish and that his resolution to remain free had given way to the intensity of his desire for her.

Smiling, she recalled that first night in his apartment when he had carried her to the couch. After she had got home that night, she had remained awake for hours, reliving the thrill of those moments. She had been delightfully stirred—not sexually—but by the knowledge that she could drive a man like Mike past the point of reason, and then force him to abject apology.

She was sure of herself, now. Mike wasn't like most of the other men she had known, men who could be kept in their place with simply a look of innocent appeal. The fact that she could control him meant that she really must be quite a girl.

Oh, she was on her way. It had taken only a little more than a month. She would be married long before Aunt Agatha returned. There would be no more living with that tight-fisted, twisted bitch; there would be no more wondering about how much longer she would last in that Washington Street mansion. There were no blood ties between her and the perverted woman who had offered her a home the year before, saying, "Your stepfather was my favorite brother, Eve. There was always a bond between us. And since both he and your mother are dead, I feel it incumbent upon me to take you in …."

Fleetingly, now, Eve thought of her mother. *Don't wait like I did, Eve. Don't wait until you're thirty to find out that a girl can get anything she wants—if she uses her body a little, and her head a lot. If I'd only known earlier!* If mother had known, she wouldn't have waited until she was past thirty and had to settle for a man like John Tremaine whose money was doled out to him by sister Agatha.

Agatha. What a scheming and wicked woman, thought Eve. Although close to fifty years of age, and a prominent figure in the type of local society founded upon wealth and possessions, in her private life, her very private life, Aunt Agatha departed from custom and conservatism. Perhaps this was because, as a girl, she had attended private schools in England, where pretty young things can pick up some surprising habits.

Oh, Aunt Agatha had once been pretty enough. Eve conceded that. The old shrew still retained a bright eye, lovely long hair as blonde as Eve's own, a skin clear as milk, and a quite youthful if rather voluptuous figure. To her circle of friends and acquaintances, dating back over the years, it was still a surprise that Agatha had never married. To Eve, however, there was no longer any mystery about Agatha's unwedded state. Eve had quickly discovered that Agatha, for peculiar reasons of her own, preferred no male attachments.

The discovery had begun on the third or fourth night after Eve had moved into Agatha's mansion.

At about two in the morning, Eve awoke with a start out of a sound sleep. It seemed to her that she had heard a scream. Sitting up in bed, she listened hard. Yes—another scream—and sounds of scuffling, strange thumpings—

In thorough alarm, Eve sprang from bed. She did not even pause to throw something over her shortie nightgown. She ran into the hall, where a dim night-light burned, paused barefoot on the thick carpet to listen again. The sounds seemed to be coming from a room upstairs. Although frightened, Eve was bent on investigating. She plunged up the stairs, located the room from which the noises were emanating, flung open the door.

The sight which greeted her was strange beyond any she had ever imagined, even in nightmares.

The room was carpeted in velvety beige, but otherwise bare except for an old-fashioned oak desk, a chair also of oak, and an incongruously luxurious, ultra-wide, ultra-soft settee covered with a red corduroy throw and supporting a wealth of multi-colored cushions. A single ceiling fixture shed a purplish fluorescent glare over the chocolate-brown walls, on which were hung prints of horses, horse races and fox-hunting scenes. A selection of curious riding crops and quirts hung on hooks along one wall. Above it, a long shelf displayed various loving cups and trophies apparently acquired at hunts and shows. Another shelf supported a selection of books about horses, and such sports as polo, steeplechasing and flat racing.

These wall adornments did not surprise Eve. Her aunt was one of the "horsy" set and a well known equestrienne at West Coast shows. The thing that was surprising was that one of the crops was missing from its hook. Aunt Agatha had it in her hand. And with it she was belaboring the bared back of a Mexican lass called Conchita.

The girl was on her knees, bent over the red couch. She was shrieking and sobbing. Eve recognized her instantly as the maid who did the housework. As Eve stood astounded, Agatha, who had heard the door opening, stayed her hand and turned.

"Eve!"

"What in the world is going on here, Aunt Agatha?"

"Step in, and shut the door. I thought you were sleeping."

"I was, but the noise woke me. Agatha, are you crazy? Why are you beating her?" Eve could not figure out the meaning of the scene, but her reaction was less that it was wrong than that it was dangerous. Coldly she said to her aunt, "Don't you realize you can be arrested for such things?"

"Oh, I can, can I?" Agatha laughed harshly. "Well, I won't be arrested on the word of this—this wench. She came in with a party of wetbacks, and if she opens her mouth, she'll be sent back across the border or into jail. If it weren't for me, she'd be out in the street where I found her, whoring for a living. I took her in. I gave her decent work, decent pay, and decent quarters. And do you know my reward? I found her here in my own private study—poking around in the desk. Looking for money—papers—God knows what!"

"And that's why you're punishing her?"

"Of course. Does she deserve to be whipped, or doesn't she?"

This put another light on matters. It wasn't just that the girl merited punishment; she could be punished without fear of reprisal.

Eve looked at her aunt, standing erect and indignant in a costume of old-fashioned white cotton nightgown, complete with eyelets at the neck and blue-ribbon drawstring at the waist. Her fleshy breasts moved quite firmly in rhythm with her angry breathing. Her figure, though well-padded, was muscular rather than plump, and her long legs, faintly pink beneath the cotton, were as straight and slim as an adolescent's. Not bad for an old maid, Eve thought, and turned to look at Conchita, who had risen from the floor. The Mexican girl had on carpet slippers, no stockings, a black skirt, and had been wearing a man's shirt, which had been pulled back from her shoulders so that now it hung about her waist. Her skin was soft, smooth, and of a lovely ecrue hue. Eve was surprised that the riding crop had left no mark upon that glowing skin. Conchita was well formed and shapely, with a beautiful bust, but she was a pretty husky specimen; there was a certain stockiness to her, and plenty of muscle. Her face had to be called attractive, Eve conceded, with its frame of dark hair, its flashing obsidian eyes, its luscious, red mouth. The expression, as Conchita regarded Agatha, was one of scorn, contempt and—yes—amusement!

"Yes, she deserves it," Eve said coldly. "The sneaking little thief. Go ahead, Agatha. Whip her."

Agatha swung, and the girl howled, falling back to the bed. She made a great to-do of it, writhing and shrieking as each blow struck her, lashing her legs about and contorting her shoulders.

Eve watched, utterly fascinated. Standing erect and tense in her nightie, she felt strange tinglings in her blood.

But at this point she considered it the better part of valor to retire. She backed out of the room, walked down the stairs, and sought the shelter of her bed on the floor below.

After a while, the noises overhead ceased. But as Eve lay in the darkness, disturbed by an excitement she did not comprehend but which would not let her sleep, she thought she heard the door open. Dimly she made out someone walking toward the bed, and then sitting down on the edge of it. Sitting down, uninvited, right next to Eve lying prone and queerly fearful. Then Eve heard a voice. It was not, as Eve had expected, the voice of her aunt.

"Do not scream," came the husky words. "It is me. Conchita."

"What do you want?"

"What I want? I want you to know *verdad*—the truth, *entiende?*"

"The truth. That's a laugh. From an ungrateful crook like you?"

"I am not a crook," said Conchita, without anger but with great pride. "Is what I come to explain. Is what I want you to know. Border jumper, *si*. Prostitute, *si*. But crook, no. Nor liar, *senorita*."

"Then why was she beating you? Why did you stand for it?"

"She do that because it is her way, *verdad?* I stand for it because she pay me well—many dollars. But I leave tomorrow, for when she tell you I am thief, that is too much. I did not sneak into that room of hers—she ordered me into it! *Si*, I leave, *senorita*. If police catch me and send me back to Mexico, maybe is for best. *Quien sabe?*"

Eve tried to get the picture. But she was more puzzled than ever. "You say it is my aunt's way to—to beat you. Conchita, if you weren't doing anything wrong, why would she want to use that riding crop on you?"

"She do not prefer the man, *entiende?* She prefer the pretty girl, like me. And she want to conquer, to master, to give pain. She has special crop, soft split leather that do not leave mark. Then afterward she ...."

"Yes?"

In the soft darkness, the word hung like a lazy echo. Eve felt the stir of Conchita's body next to her own on the bed; she felt the warmness of Conchita, smelled the aromatic essences of her lovely hair, the cinnamon of her healthy skin. Trembling on the verge of mysteries, Eve was fearful no longer. Only the obscure excitement remained. And the poignant question.

As if in answer, Conchita sighed. She too was agitated, and unable to restrain herself, she reached out her hand and stroked Eve's golden curls.

"I show you," Conchita said huskily.

Her rosy lips found Eve's hot, dry mouth ....

Eve felt Mike's arm tighten about her shoulders. He didn't have nearly as much money as she would like, but the past year with Aunt Agatha had opened her eyes. There were so few young men who were wealthy and at the same time unmarried. But this way, she would be able to acquire her own wealth. Besides, wealth was only part of it. To be a glamorous celebrity, envied and idolized, recognized—that was what she wanted.

Mike would be able to push aside the obstacles that were bound to confront her on the road to success. He was clever. No doubt about that. Also, he had the knack of teaching. He even knew how to make practice seem like fun instead of the drudgery it had always been before. He had imagination and verve. He was just the right man for her—for the time being, anyway.

She saw the tip of his cigarette flair and then describe a red arc as he flung it from the car. His face moved closer to hers.

"Eve, I'm in love with you. You know that, of course. And I think you care for me. Do you, darling? Tell me—"

"I've loved you from almost the first moment I saw you, Mike." It was perfectly safe to say something like that. She laughed inwardly.

"And you will marry me, darling?"

"Yes, Mike."

Hungrily, his mouth sought hers, his breath rasping. His hand slipped beneath her coat and he shoved his fingers inside her dress, seeking her breast. Under the chafing touch, the nipple hardened.

"Mike—" she protested.

"It's all right, darling. We're going to be married!" His hands became more eager and she pulled away from him with a shocked cry.

"Sorry, Eve," he muttered thickly. He straightened and reached for a cigarette.

She put her face on his shoulder. "Don't you understand, Mike? After we're married, well—it will be different."

"I understand, Eve." But he didn't. Her lips had been so cool, her response so slight. It was as though she didn't care for him at all.

Determinedly, he forced the thought from his mind. She'd told him she loved him, hadn't she? He was simply imagining things. It was just that, subconsciously, he was still fighting the idea of marriage.

He said quickly: "We can fly to Reno tonight." He forced a quick laugh. "Get it over with before I change my mind—"

"But, Mike, I'm on the air tomorrow morning. And the next day, too. We'll have to be married here in town."

"It'll be a three-day wait."

"Why, Mike! You make it sound as though it were three years. Now, look—we can go down to City Hall and get our license some time tomorrow."

Mike wanted a drink—and quick. He started the car and drove down the winding road toward North Beach. "How about dropping in at Izzy's to celebrate?"

Eve wrinkled her little nose. "It's such a grimy place, darling! I'd rather go to the St. Francis or the Mark, but—if you really want to go to Izzy's—"

They went to the St. Francis.

"Not the cocktail lounge, Mike. I'm dying to dance."

They danced. Eve looked up at him, seemingly oblivious of the eyes that turned their way. Mike smiled. "Every man here is looking at you and you know it, you little devil!"

And he thought: *Every man is envying me. Lord, she's gorgeous. I'm damned lucky.*

By eleven o'clock, it seemed to Mike that the couples on the dance floor had merged into one large undulating entity. The music tumbled about in his brain as well as against his ears. "Another highball, waiter."

"No, Mike. Let's dance."

"Got to celebrate. Getting married—"

"That's your sixth—or maybe your seventh drink! Come on, let's dance."

He got to his feet. He didn't stagger. He never staggered. With Eve at his side, he threaded the maze of tables. He blinked, just a trifle, trying to bring the gyrating, dancing couples into focus. And then he was among them, circling, bumping, smelling perfume and bodies.

Even through the mist that swirled in front of his eyes, he could see how glorious Eve was. Just a few days more, and.... Anticipation made him tremble. He would toy with her, would slowly take off her dress and with long, caressing strokes slide the silky stuffs beneath past her lovely, rounded flesh until it gleamed in the intimate lamplight. His lips would brush against her shoulder, would linger on the petal skin, and he would rub his cheek against the soft, satiny resilience of her. Then he would carry her to the marriage bed.

They would lie there close, warm and wedded, prolonging ecstatic time...

"Mike, you're holding me too tight!"

Relaxing his embrace, he grinned apologetically.

She smiled back. "Know what, Mike? I think it would be fun to go to Izzy's."

"At this hour, the place will be a madhouse. Everybody from the station will be in for a night cap—"

"Oh." She sighed wistfully. "I thought you'd be pleased."

He was touched. She didn't like that dingy little place, but she knew how much he liked old Izzy. "You're a wonderful girl, Eve."

"The joint's jumping," Mike said as they walked into Izzy's bar.

Hank Walton's voice reached them over the clamor. "Izzy! Hey—get out the drinks for some gentlemen of note!"

"Seems like the musicians have just arrived," Mike said. A second later, he and Eve stepped into the crowded room.

"Just one drink, fellers!" warned Augie Carson, the trombone player. "Y'see, Izzy, we're going up to Manny's joint. We're giving him a surprise party for his birthday." Manny was the station's musical director.

"We ought to have some presents for him," someone said.

"We got a car full of liquor. That should be enough."

"Nope," Hank Walton put in. "Fats is right. We ought to get him something good. Tell you what, we'll go down to Chinatown and pick up a dozen of those live eels they sell down there. Buy a fancy box to put 'em in and hand it to Manny. Tell him they're neckties."

There was a chorus of approving guffaws.

"I got a street stop-sign," the cellist said. "Knocked it down at the beach last night. I'm going to put it at the foot of Manny's bed and—" He broke off, looking toward the entrance way. "Well, what do you know. Hi, Mike."

"Hi," Mike called back as he and Eve moved toward the bar.

Hank Walton shouted, "How about you kids coming along? To coin a phrase—the more the merrier."

"Not tonight," Mike said.

"No, not tonight," Eve's clear voice rang out. "Mike and I have something of our own to celebrate. Our engagement."

The back-thumping commenced and Mike listened to the good-natured raillery:

So, the smart guy who said he'd never get hooked ain't no smarter than the rest of us, huh?

Hell, what can a gal like Eve see in a chump like you?

And, Augie Carson: *Well, the gal has plenty of witnesses. You try backing out, and she can sue you for breach of promise.*

Hank Walton nudged Mike in the ribs. "Don't look so glum, chum. Breach of promise suits have been outlawed in this state for years."

Mike had managed to hold the grin on his lips. But, the moment the trombone player had spoken, the thought flashed into his mind: Was that why Eve suggested coming to Izzy's? So that he would be publicly committed, so that he couldn't back out without looking like a jerk?

"Scotch, Izzy. Scotch in a beer glass."

He couldn't back out now, not decently. But would he have wanted to? Hadn't he thought it all out reasonably? Still, maybe Eve had sensed his curious disquiet after he had tried to make love to her on Telegraph Hill, and maybe—

"Another scotch, Izzy."

"You maybe had too much already, no?"

"Never had too much. There isn't that much."

"I dunno." The worried host hesitated.

"Izzy, you old walrus! Eve and I are going to get married. Sleep together legally. Music. Nickel in the slot machine—Got to dance—"

"Pour me another, Izzy. Lucky guy, aren't I? Going to get married. All legal. God and government will approve."

CHAPTER FIVE

A SHOWER and ten grains of aspirin partially revived Mike the next morning. He switched on the electric percolator in the hope that a couple of cups of scalding coffee might dissolve the fur that seemed to have sprouted around his tonsils. Waiting for the coffee, he sat at the dinette table, holding his head in his hands. He'd got engaged, last night. He remembered that much. And, he could remember everything pretty well up to his third scotch at Izzy's.

After that... He let out a dismal groan. If only he were like Hank Walton, for instance, who began staggering and mumbling when he got really loaded, then bartenders would either refuse to serve him or would water down the scotch. But, damn it, he, Mike, could walk straight and talk straight even when he was approaching absolute unconsciousness. He'd stay on his feet and his mouth would work automatically, and sensible sounding words would come out.

He poured the coffee. Black and bitter—like his thoughts. He asked himself: *Why do I drink so much? I'm supposed to have brains. Brilliant—that's what they called me at college.*

Why do I drink? Because liquor provides an escape from reality? Is it that I'm actually afraid of reality? Is that why I've tried to avoid marriage? Haven't I the courage to face reality?

His jaws tensed. Well, he was going to meet reality head on, from here on out. Married to Eve, everything would be different. He'd look at things straight, clearheaded and clear-eyed.

Now he could analyze that feeling of apprehension he had known in the car when he had tried to jump the gun. He had still been struggling to avoid the responsibilities of more mature living. That's why he had imagined she was cold; that was why he had mentally accused her of trapping him when she had made that announcement at Izzie's.

He finished a second cup of coffee and then frowned at his watch. Time to leave.

On his way to the station, his thoughts turned uneasily to Sally Kaye. She had always insisted that he was free to leave her whenever he wanted to, but—she should have been the first to know. He should have told her. Sally, who had been so sweet, so understanding, so stimulating and—so passionate. There would never be anyone like this dark willowy girl whose quiet beauty had intrigued him from the start. She wasn't spectacular like Eve, but—

He remembered how he had felt the first time he had met her, how he had gasped, "God, you're a lovely creature."

And she had said with a little smile, "Same to you, mister." About an hour later, she had said, "I think we'd be good for each other."

"You don't happen to mean—?"

"That's exactly what I mean."

He hadn't had the apartment, then. They had gone to a downtown hotel. He would never forget that night, nor would he forget all the other nights since. There would never be another girl like Sally. Only thing was, he had never wanted to marry her. And he didn't want to marry her now. He wanted to marry Eve.

Turning into the studios, he saw Sally in the corridor. Her dark eyes were too bright, maybe because of the tears she was holding back.

He swore under his breath. He should have called her, told her of his decision to marry Eve. Sally should have been the first to know. She would have been prepared, then. She could have contrived a smile to wear through the long hours of the day ahead. But now—humiliation was added to her heartbreak. He watched her hurry into her office.

As Mike walked on, he acknowledged with a nod or a wave of the hand the greetings of the others.

Manny Rhodes shouted, "Congratulations, Mike."

Mary Sweet: "I hope you and Eve will be marvelously happy, I really do."

Hazzard, excitedly: "Mike, we'll make it a radio wedding, see? Put it on the *Variety Show.* I'll arrange everything…no? But, Mike, think of the publicity! Eve can use it."

A while later, Mike unobtrusively stepped into Sally's office. She looked up and said, "Good luck, Mike. I hope you'll be awfully happy. I really mean it."

"I should have called you last night. I didn't want you to get it second-hand. But, hell—I was drinking, and—"

"It's all right, Mike."

"It isn't all right. I feel rotten about it. If I hadn't been so busy feeling sorry for myself this morning, I'd have thought to have phoned you—"

"You don't have to make a production out of it. I said it's all right. Forget it. You'd better leave now."

"You'll have lunch with me?"

She shook her head. "No more lunches, no more dinners."

"Sally. There's no reason we can't go on being friends—"

"In the first place, I don't think Eve would approve, Mike."

"Why not? What's wrong about it? In this day and age, a man can have women friends, can't he?"

She smiled wryly. "You're overlooking something, Mike. We've been lovers as well as friends. Do you think we could keep in mind that point where friendliness leaves off and loving begins? It has to be 'voir, my darling."

He was aghast at the thought of not seeing her as he had in the past, not having those good talks, not hearing her laughter— and not ever making love to her again.

"Please go, Mike."

Manny Rhodes stopped by Mike's office. His thin, mobile face was alight with interest. "Say, is it really true that Eve is moving over to Continental next month?"

Mike nodded.

Manny went on, "I saw Terris coming out of your office. Did he finally talk you into moving over to Continental, too?"

"I'm sticking it out here a while longer, Manny. At Continental, I'd be just another obscure producer. Here, I do get my name in the papers now and then. Occasionally, I'm able to talk Hazzard into letting me put on something different and I get noticed. So, that's why I'm hanging around. I'm waiting for something better than a routine production job. As for Eve—"

He had tried to persuade her to wait for a better offer, but she had been so excited and eager. And he had thought: Well, we'll be married before she goes over to Continental and I'll be able to watch out for her.

"You'd make a lot more money over at Continental, Mike."

"Maybe so. But I'd be just one of a dozen, struggling and pushing, and kicking my way up. I doubt if you know a single one of that network's producers by name. All they do is stand around with a stopwatch and make signs. Maybe they're necessary to get the program on and off on time, but who ever hears of them?"

"They do some writing. And that's what you want to do, don't you?"

"I am writing." Mike thought of the television script he had just sold. The first—but there'd be more. "I've time to do a little stuff on my own. But over at Continental, they'd keep me busy turning out that drivel of theirs. For instance, the crud they put on between musical selections."

Manny grinned. "You don't think much of that too, too cute stuff, huh?"

"Why can't the announcer simply mention the name of the number about to be played."

"I'd go for that myself." Manny sighed. "Of course, I'm prejudiced, but I figure that people who tune in for a musical program don't want to listen to a lot of yak the producers call 'continuity' but I call 'crap.' The commercials are bad enough."

The telephone on Mike's desk rang. "Mike?"

It was Hank Walton. "Look, Mike, got something on my program today that'll give you a kick. Be sure and catch it."

"Okay, Hank."

Mike had an idea as to what it would be. Something that had to do with his engagement to Eve. Something which Hank would consider colossal.

Just before three o'clock, Mike went into the control room and sat down in the booth with the technician. He looked out at the people who were milling around the studio.

Manny Rhodes, on the square platform which served as the conductor's stand, was squeezing in a last-second rehearsal while Hank Walton, shuffling papers in his hand, shouted orders. Mary Sweet was talking animatedly with Tony Ransford, the new tenor.

In another booth, a station announcer with his hand to his ear, intoned, "Five o'clock. Time to get that loan on your car ... easy payments ... the Nabb way is the honest way ... "

Then Studio A was suddenly transformed from an arena of maniacs to a roomful of dummies. Hank Walton fixed his gaze on the second hand of the studio clock. Manny Rhodes' baton was raised. Five seconds ... two seconds ... the technician, mixing the program with lightning fingers, pressed a series of buttons. Relays clicked and the red light gleamed.

Manny brought down his baton. Fanfare. Then he made appealing gestures for softer notes. Pianissimo. Voice background.

Hank Walton began speaking into the microphone.

Mike listened. As an emcee, Hank was all right. He had a penchant for words. A knack. If necessary, he could talk for hours.

Mike, his chin cupped in his hand, watching from the control room, wondered how the invisible audience visualized Hank Walton. Did the listening housewives have some image of him?

Oh, it wasn't likely they were paying much attention. They'd be peeling potatoes about this time, lifting the lid to look at the pot roast, getting dinner ready for the old man.

Mike squirmed. All those drab, middle-class husbands. Once some of them had been bright young men. Now they were dull plodders, never daring to take a gamble once they had accepted the responsibility of a wife and family.

Stop thinking such things, you damned fool, Mike told himself.

Hank was concluding: And now—on with the Women's Newspaper."

The Women's Newspaper invaded the ether lanes three days a week. Designed primarily to catch the interest of a feminine audience, it skirted dangerous reefs. On its first voyage, the show traveled fast. But, on each succeeding trip, it had carried an additional burden of commercial freight. The speed had slackened. One day, it would sink with all hands, Mike reflected.

"Topics of the day—" Hank was saying. He mentioned his birthday, a little hint to listening housewives. Then: "Now, here we have a story with a happy ending. Or, perhaps I should say, a happy beginning, at least. Eve, come over here."

Mike leaned forward. How exquisite she was.

"Eve," Hank said, "it's been rumored that you and our genial program manager, Mike Carlyle, are going to ankle it to the altar. Is that correct?"

"Quite correct," she replied.

"Ha! Romance right here in the studios, folks. And spring's over, too. Eve, tell us how you felt when Mike popped the question. I bet you were surprised. Everybody knows Mike is—was—a confirmed bachelor."

"Oh, I wasn't surprised. You see—he had been wooing me."

The musicians were grinning at Mike through the studio window. He flushed. He glowered angrily at the technician, who was snickering. Damn Walton, he thought.

"And when did he pop the question, Eve?"

"Last night. Mike parked up on Telegraph Hill and after about an hour—"

The musicians howled. It was obvious what they and perhaps the listening audience were thinking. More than a proposal might have taken place in that parked car.

Walton, that bastard. Giving Eve lines like that.

Mike stalked out of the control room and went back to his office.

He told Eve afterward: "It was cheap. Rotten bad taste."

"But, Mike, what was wrong with it?"

She didn't understand.

With a wistful smile, she went on: "It was publicity, wasn't it? And isn't that what I need?"

He took a long breath. "I'm going to have to teach you so many things, my little Eve."

CHAPTER SIX

EVE HAD been spending every spare moment shopping. "The upholstery is eggshell white satin and—"

"Just a moment, Eve. We can't use all that stuff in my apartment."

"Of course not, darling. I found this perfectly lovely place early this afternoon and I put down a deposit. Now—getting back to the furniture. Your hi-fi combination is good, but your piano simply will not do. We'll rent a grand."

He smiled at her excitement. Like a youngster she was, buying new toys. And yet, efficient too. Knowing exactly what she wanted—and getting it.

He said, "Tomorrow, this time, we'll be in Carmel." They would have two days together. Too short a time for a honeymoon, really, Mike thought. But they both had program schedules. Radio audiences didn't take honeymoons into account when shows failed to appear. The mystery serial Mike wrote had to go on so that a certain brand of shaving cream could be extolled; the *Variety Show* couldn't skip a week; and Betty and Benny had to cavort.

Although Eve backed up Harry Hazzard, there was no radio wedding. It was a very quiet affair with just Ted O'Neill and Manny Rhodes as witnesses.

With Eve close by his side, Mike drove down the coast highway to Carmel. The short, simple ceremony had affected him profoundly.

Do you take this woman— Again, the words echoed solemnly in his mind. He heard himself saying, "I never realized it before, Eve. But marriage is important and—"

"Why, certainly," she said. Then: "I've been thinking, why don't we stay at the Lodge instead of going on to Carmel?"

"But we want to go where it's quiet, don't we? Where we can get away from people. Anyway, we'd have had to make reservations."

"Yes, I suppose so." There was no missing the note of disappointment.

They registered at the inn among the cypresses and Mike felt slightly queer and at the same time very honorable as he wrote: *Mr. and Mrs. Michael Carlyle* in the register. He eyed the clerk narrowly, wondering if the man suspected they were a couple seeking illicit pleasure. But the clerk was smiling respectfully. Mike thought: He knows. It must be that these fellows can spot the decently married pairs.

Proudly, Mike took Eve's arm and followed the bellboy.

At last they were alone, and in a cheerful, comfortable room. Mike turned to Eve. This was the moment for which he had waited so long. He moved toward her.

She had turned, was opening her suitcase. "If I don't get everything unpacked in a hurry, my clothes will be ruined."

He watched silently as she lifted out a sheer dinner dress and carefully placed it on a hanger in the closet. Then there was the business of shaking the wrinkles out of a skirt, smoothing a blouse, brushing a suit.

Mike thought: She's making a ritual out of the thing. He opened his own bag. There, on top, was the fifth of scotch Manny had forced on him. He hadn't intended to do any drinking, but he was edgy. A drink. Just one drink surely would not harm.

He went into the bathroom and poured out a good slug. "Want a drink, Eve?"

"Not now, Mike. And—please shut that door and stay in there for a couple of minutes. I'm getting undressed."

It wasn't as he had planned it, but if this was the way she wanted it … He smiled. He took off his coat and flung it over the towel rack. His fingers trembled as he undid his tie.

A moment passed. And another. "Eye?" he called through the bathroom door.

"Just one second more, darling."

It was unendurable. He reached for the tumbler, gulped down the drink.

Then:

"You can come in now, Mike—"

He didn't see her at first; his eyes had gone to the bed. And she was standing by the window, every perfect curve of her body utterly revealed.

She looked toward him and gasped. "Mike! Whatever are you thinking of! Coming in like that—stark naked."

He was blinking stupidly, looking at the exquisite body tightly sheathed in a scarlet bathing suit.

She had averted her eyes. "I put your beach things on the chair."

Automatically, he reached down for his trunks and terry-cloth robe. Wordlessly, he returned to the bathroom. Before he rejoined her, he took another drink—a big one.

He was angry. Not with her but with himself, he thought, as they went down the path to the beach. He should have kept in mind that she was just a very young girl—unawakened. In her mind, a honeymoon was a kind of romantic vacation, a time to play and swim and dance and, at the proper time—bedtime—go to bed.

They swam in the gentle surf and then lay side by side on the white sand. She talked of the days ahead when she would be over at Continental. "Tell me, just what is the set-up over there? Is Terris really the top man?"

Mike, lying on his stomach, vainly trying to put down the erotic thoughts which tormented him, murmured, "What's that, Eve?"

She repeated her question.

"No doubt about Terris being top dog. He's big stuff, and he knows it."

"You sound as though you don't like him, Mike."

"I don't." As he replied, he realized that this was the thing to do: talk shop, get everything else out of his head. And so, he spoke at length, and he told her what he knew about the big network's TV operations.

She was entranced. "It's fascinating, Mike."

"It's a rat-race."

"I don't think so, Mike. If you simply use your head."

"And keep a knife handy. A nice sharp knife to cut yourself a piece of throat with."

"Naturally," she said quietly.

He looked at her quickly. She wasn't smiling. So, she wasn't joking about it. But when he looked deeply into her candid blue eyes, he became completely confident she had spoken out of sheer artlessness. She just didn't understand.

She lingered over dinner a long time. She's scared, Mike told himself. She's pretending to be so nonchalant, but—If only he could dredge up the right words and phrases. If he could find some way to tell her that she had nothing to fear, that he would be gentle. And he would be. He'd hold his wild ardor in check.

"We've had a long day, darling" he said softly. "Don't you think—?"

"Yes," she said, rising from the table. "But my fatigue isn't only because of today. All that running around, finding the apartment and attending to the shopping. . . . I'm actually worn out."

She looked up at him beseechingly when they were back in their room. "Mike, even if we are married, I'd rather not undress in front of you."

"I'll go in the bathroom."

"No, Mike. I'll go. I'll take my things in there and I'll be with you in just a little while."

He lay in bed, waiting. He willed himself to be patient, reminding himself of his resolve: Tonight he would think only of her; gently, he would teach her the art of love which, afterwards, they would practice with mutual dedication.

Then, finally, he saw her step from the bathroom. How much the bride she looked in the filmy white gown! She switched off the lamp on the bedside table and then slipped beneath the covers.

His lips touched hers tenderly and his hands caressed her cool, smooth flesh. "My dearest," he murmured, breathing kisses into her breasts, lightly caressing her lithe, magnificent curves.

Moments passed.

Eve said, "Mike, I'm awfully tired. If you are going to—I mean—"

Was this her shy way of telling him that she was aroused? That she wanted him? Of course it was. It had to be.

She yielded to his ardor. Another moment passed. She cried out softly, briefly.

"Darling!" he whispered.

"It's all right, Mike," she said calmly, her body relaxing. She lay very still in his arms.

A few moments passed.

Then suddenly she got up and hurried to the bathroom. He stared at the thin line of light at the bottom of the door. He had failed her utterly. Not even for a fleeting second had he given her any pleasure.

Mike looked over the mail on his desk. Nothing important. And everything was running smoothly enough at the station. It would be just another routine day. But tonight there would be home, and Eve.

Eve. Suddenly he remembered what, in his perplexity, he had asked her during the ride back from Carmel.

"Darling, tell me something."

"Yes, Mike?"

"Do you enjoy it when I kiss you?"

"Of course, Mike."

That had been all. She had gone back to what to her was apparently a more important subject—her future with Continental.

He found himself, now, comparing her to other women he had known. In particular, Sally. What a delight it had always been to touch Sally. A delight communicated to her and shared by her. To him, it had been an ever-fascinating phenomenon, a glowing warmth growing by degree into a white-hot passion and, after that, exquisite consummation.

With Eve, it was different. He was frustrated and, at the same time, compensated. For not a man in ten thousand could boast of a more beautiful wife. And, along with her beauty, she had genuine talent. They would go places together. They were ideally matched. And there was really no physiological problem. It was just that she had not yet been awakened. She was young. And she wasn't one of those tramps who indulge in casual couplings from the time they're in high school. Naturally, it would take help and patience to cultivate the passion he wished to evoke in her.

He turned to his typewriter. This was no time to dawdle. There was the Betty and Benny show to prepare. He scowled. At first he had liked this young married couple he had created. But by now he had lost all affection for them. They just bored him.

Harry Hazzard poked his head into the office. "Got those blackouts ready for the *Variety Show*?"

"Not yet. You know how it is. Haven't been able to get around to them. Been too busy being a new husband."

Hazzard leered. "A gal like Eve ought to stimulate your imagination. She'd heat up a marble statue." Noting Mike's frown, he cleared his throat. "Anyway, try to get those blackouts ready so

I can okay them. Oh, another thing. I told Sally to drop in. Give her something she can use for a publicity release. Something like, well, you and Eve got stopped by a traffic cop on your way to Carmel and Eve says something cute. You know, the kind of stuff that might make one of the big columns." He looked over his shoulder. "She's coming now. Okay, Mike. Be seein' you."

Sally walked in then, came toward his desk saying, "Thought you'd have enough to do catching up with your regular chores, so I've cooked up a couple of so-called bright sayings. Look them over and—" She dropped the paper on his desk and sat down in the chair opposite him.

He read the typewritten lines. It was a damned thoughtful thing for her to have done, he reflected. He didn't deserve any consideration from her.

"Both of these are good, Sally. Really good." Not a hint of bad taste or cheapness. They were clever. She'd worked hard on these quips. He knew enough about the business of humor to know that. "I can't choose between them. They're both swell, Sally. I can't tell you how much I appreciate it." He looked at her.

She was sitting there, legs crossed. Long, slender, perfectly proportioned legs. His body began tingling. "Sally—"

She stood up. "Well, since you haven't any preference, I'll use the first one, Mike." She started toward the door.

"Wait a minute, Sally."

She glanced back. "If it's about Manny Rhodes' party tonight, I told him I was sorry but I couldn't make it." The door closed behind her.

He'd forgotten all about the party Manny was throwing for him and Eve. Manny had said, "See if you can round up Ted O'Neill. I haven't been able to get in touch with him." Mike reached for the telephone.

Mike heard Ted's voice coming the wire, "Nobody's been able to catch up with me, boy. One of those irons I had on the fire down south heated up ahead of schedule and I've been trying to clean up things at this end. I'm flying to L. A. So tonight's clambake is out. Anyway, give my best to Sal—I mean Eve. And, as soon as I'm halfway settled, I'll drop you a line."

At home, dressing for the party, Eve said, "Terris has his eye on you. I talked with him today. I think you really should go over to Continental."

Mike smiled tolerantly. Eve wanted to light the fuse which would send him rocketing. And she could, he thought. With her beside him, he was no longer earth-bound. Together, they'd ride to the stars.

CHAPTER SEVEN

MIKE AND Eve arrived at Manny Rhodes' apartment a little after nine. They were the first to arrive with the exception of Hank Walton, who had been there for an hour. He had lowered the tide considerably on a bottle of bourbon.

Ulrica Rhodes, a plump German singer Manny had brought back from Berlin, led Eve down the hall to take off her wraps. Almost immediately after they returned to the spacious drawing room, other guests began arriving.

First there was Mary Sweet, clinging to Tony Ransford's arm. Then, Harry Hazzard, coming in alone and more than a little tipsy. He was singing, off key, "Here comes the bride—"

Someone said, "Give him another drink, Manny. Maybe that'll shut him up."

"Listen, Mike," Manny said, "Terris is dropping by later."

Harry had kissed Eve, was turning to Mike. "I feel so good I'd kiss you too, but—" he giggled—"but brunettes don't agree with me. Hank, kiss him for me. Hank—where's Hank?"

Mike swung away hastily and made for the little bar. He didn't want Hank slobbering all over him.

Mary Sweet was sipping sherry at the bar. "Oh, let me be bar-maid," she said, an inviting look in her eyes as she smiled up at Mike. She began pouring the scotch.

"Whoa," Mike protested. "I'm taking it easy tonight, Mary." But he hadn't spoken soon enough. He frowned at the glass. There were a good four ounces there, he thought. Well, after this one, he'd go light.

"Have another shot, Mike."

"Look, Manny—"

"Don't argue, sweetheart. This is a big night."

"A big night is right," Hank shouted. "Roll me in crumbs, mother, I'm going to get fried."

Words beat against the walls. Cigarette stubs slipped over the edges of trays and the ashes mingled with the sticky rings on the blonde furniture. The radio began blaring: "Ay-round the corner—"

Voices:

Who's that? Yeah? Well, he's lousy. All right, he's making the dough, but he still stinks. Don't you think so, Mike?

Hey, Mike—can I borrow your woman?

Has she got any sisters, Mike?

Mike glanced down at the glass in his hand. A moment ago, it had been full, but now—

New arrivals. Couldn't distinguish their faces too well. Everything was kind of hazy. Must be the smoke.

"Hi—you remember me, don't you, Mike?" And then, Manny was bringing more people around and Ulrica was babbling away in her richly accented voice, "Effer-body looves Mike."

Another glass was thrust into his hand. He was drinking automatically now. His eyes were on Eve. She was dancing with Tony Ransford. Not a bad-looking guy, young Ransford. And women were beginning to go crazy about his voice.

Behind him, Augie Carson was saying, "Watch your step, Hank. Make another pass like that at my girl and—"

Then, a sudden hush came over the drawing room. Terris, of the Continental web, had put in an appearance. He looked like the big wheel he was: could pose any day for a collar or shirt advertisement. Square and slightly florid face, silvery gray hair.

At Terris' side was a stunning redhead, a bit flamboyant.

Harvey Terris pulled away from the crowd, strode toward Mike with his hand outstretched. For a while, he spoke in generalities and then: We could use you over at Continental, Carlyle. It'd mean you'd be switching media but I understand you've been doing considerable TV writing and—" His eyes strayed. Following the direction of his gaze, Mike saw that Terris was looking at Eve. But then, what man wasn't? She was breathtakingly lovely in that strapless gown of a hue matching her sapphire eyes.

She freed herself from Ransford's arm and hurried to Mike and Terris. "Hello, Harvey."

"Nice to see you, Eve."

Harvey. Eve. Mike's brows drew closer together. Terris wasn't the kind of man who went in for easy familiarity at gatherings like these. He called men by their last names; women—with certain exceptions—he invariably addressed as Miss or Mrs.

"Eve," Harvey Terris said, "I've been trying to persuade your husband to come over to Continental." Then, he turned back to Mike. "That Betty and Benny script of yours has TV possibilities. I caught it last week. It seems to me—"

Hank Walton, sobered by the prospect of meeting the great man, had straightened up, was making his way toward Mike with an air of expectancy.

Mike introduced him. Hank said, "Mr. Terris, I just had to come over here to tell you that the *Crackpot Carnival* show is the greatest thing on the air!"

"Thanks, Walton," Terris said. "We've been rather expecting a good rating."

"Lemme get you a drink. Scotch?"

"Thank you, no. I have one." Terris then turned to Eve.

But Hank wasn't to be corked. "Ever catch my Women's Newspaper of the Air?" He wedged his way past Mike.

Mike made it easy for him. He stepped back a pace and whispered to Eve, "Let's dance."

As they swayed in rhythm to the music, Mike said, "Did you ask Terris to catch Betty and Benny?"

Her eyes were alight with satisfaction. "That I did. And, he caught it, didn't he? I thought he would, but I didn't want to say anything to you until I was sure. When we go back, I'll see to it that Hank moves out of the picture, even if I have to dance with the oaf. But, I want you to have a talk with Harvey. I have the strongest feeling that he's about to offer you something good, with a really big salary! And, Mike—"

"Well?"

"It's just this, Mike. Harvey says he has got the impression you don't like him."

"Frankly, I don't. I respect his ability, but—"

"Be nice to him, Mike!"

"You mean, butter him up like Hank is doing? See here, darling. I don't go around wagging my tail for a bone."

"Silly boy. What difference does it make what you do, just so long as you get ahead?"

"You don't know what you're saying, darling." He looked down into her face. What a child she was. A child mouthing words she liked the sound of, having not the slightest comprehension of their real meaning.

Harry Hazzard, dancing with the redhead who had come with Terris, called out, "Mike, look what I've got."

Eve asked softly, "Who's that girl, Mike?"

"Lola something-or-other. She's been singing at the Club Capri. Terris got her into a couple of video shows but she doesn't seem to click. She hasn't enough of a voice for just radio, but Harry's probably promising to put her on the air."

"Did you see Harry's wife? She came in just a while ago, all by herself. She's over there, talking with Ulrica." Eve inclined her head.

Mike looked over toward the archway. Nadine Hazzard was standing there, her body rigid, her face pale and strained. "She sure looks like hell," he muttered, wondering why a nice girl like Nadine was still in such an agony of indecision about divorcing that bantam rooster. It seemed impossible that any girl could care for Harry Hazzard, but then, women were funny.

Eve said, "They say that she took an overdose of sleeping pills when she found out about that place where Harry takes girls who have radio ambitions. But the ambulance got her in time."

The station musicians, their work for the day finished, had begun augmenting the crowd. Max Ralley, the staff pianist, sat down at the piano and began tearing away at a Cole Porter number.

"Give us some ricky-tik, Max."

"Play something hot, Maxie."

"We wanna dance."

Mary Sweet, putting her arm about Max, began crooning. "Night and day—"

"Mike," Eve said insistently, "go over there and talk to Harvey."

"No."

"And why not?"

"Well." He hesitated, "There's something about it that doesn't hit me right. Sure, I've been holding out for something better than a routine producing job, and Terris knows it. But, he had a look in his eyes tonight which led me to believe he was going to offer something big."

"And isn't that just what you want?"

"Yes, but I want to get it on my own merits—not my wife's."

"Mike, don't be a fool." She sounded exasperated. "We need the money, don't we?"

"Not that bad."

"For the last time, are you going to have a talk with him?"

"No," he said flatly. "I'm going to have a drink."

He missed the scornful look she gave him as he started toward the bar.

Midnight.

"Hi, Mike. You're cold sober. Have another drink. What's that, Augie? Sure, he's got a hollow leg, but one of these days we'll get him drunk, won't we, boy?"

I feel pretty good. Warm and relaxed. One more drink and I'll be feeling really high. "Thanks, Manny. What's that, Augie? Sure, I can say 'United States twin screw steel cruisers.'"

"What a guy."

"I'll say he is!" That was the redhead. She squealed, "Know what he said to me. For a honeymoon tonight, he'll marry me next Tuesday! He's a riot."

Mike was looking at the blurred face. "Manny, have you seen Eve?"

"I think she went up on the roof for some air."

Hazzard whooped. "She's up there counting the stars with Terris."

Mike closed one eye and things came into better focus. Terris wasn't around. Well, maybe they did need air. Who didn't? He could use some himself. Still, maybe another drink—

Behind him, he heard shouted greetings. He turned. Sally Kaye stood in the doorway. "Hello, Mike." She swayed toward him.

So she had decided to come, after all.

Her glossy hair was mussed, her lipstick smeared. He could see her very clearly—and he could see the man who was with her—and without shutting one eye, either. It was a strange thing, something which had never happened to him before, this snapping into sobriety.

That big bastard who was with her. Look at him, six feet four, if he was an inch. Broad shoulders, flat belly. A good-looking devil with black hair just a bit long at the temples, with knowing eyes and a sensuous mouth.

Sally hiccupped softly and, looking up at her escort, said, "Bruce, I want you to meet Mike Carlyle. Mike, this is Bruce Stockton."

Stockton—Mike felt his hand being crushed in a power-ful grip. *Bruce Stockton.* Then, it came to him. Stockton was the producer of the two biggest television shows coming out of Hollywood. All the eyes in the entertainment world were on him, this man in his early thirties who seemed to have inherited the Stockton brains as well as the Stockton fortune.

Sally was saying, "Ted introduced me to Bruce last week. Bruce is nice." Her voice was a little thick. "But, he'll never be able to take your place."

"I'm going to try like hell," Stockton said. He was smiling, but there was an odd note of determination in his voice.

"Have a drink, Sally." That was Manny.

She took the glass. She lifted it to her lips, tilted her head. When she put down the glass, Mike saw it was empty. Sally had never drunk like that before. He regarded Bruce Stockton narrowly.

Stockon was taking only an occasional sip.

He's making a point of staying sober; he's waiting for the psychological moment—when she's just drunk enough to say "What the hell—" And then, he'll get her into bed, and—

It was none of his business. There was no excuse for catching Hank Walton's eye, signaling him with a significant nod. "Hank, here's someone you've been wanting to meet. Bruce Stockton."

"And have I been wanting to meet you, Stockton! Man, that *Startling Stars* is the biggest thing."

"Sally," Mike steered her toward the kitchen. "We're going to have some coffee."

"Don't want coffee. 'Nother li'l drink—"

"You don't know what you're doing, Sally."

"Do too. Drowning my sorrows, that's what."

"And trying to get up enough nerve to get in the hay with Stockton."

"I don't think he's going to be so hard to take."

He pushed her down into a chromed kitchen chair. There was a gleaming electric percolator on the table. He found a cup and poured out the hot coffee.

Reluctantly, she lifted the cup. "Don't want to sober up, Mike. Want to go to Bruce's hotel. I've got to get you out of my blood, Mike. I've got to."

He looked into her face and the past assumed a kind of reality which made the present seem as unsubstantial as he drove along the beach highway, her hair touseled the stove scrambling eggs. He saw her sitting beside him as he drove along the beach highway, her hair touseled by the wind and her eyes bright with the joy of living. He saw her at her typewriter, frowning as she concentrated on her work, her fine forehead smoothing when she would look up and find him there. He thought of the look of rapture in her eyes when he held her close.

Sally finished her coffee. "No, Mike. No more. Well, all right." She smiled wanly. "Hasn't it occurred to you that you won't always be on hand to sober me up? Anyway, I'm not your responsibility any more—that is, if I ever was. You've got Eve."

Eve. He'd forgotten about Eve. She was with Terris, someone had said. His glance went to the door next to the refrigerator. That was the way up to the roof. They'd been gone a long time.

Harry Hazzard and the redheaded singer barged into the kitchen. "What a night," he howled. Then, seeing Mike and Sally, he began giggling uncontrollably. Finally subsiding, he poked the redhead in the ribs. "Take a look at that guy, Mike. Cooking things up with the old flame, and his wife's up on the roof necking with Terris. Oh, brother, you kids have beat even my record when it comes to having a short honeymoon."

"Don't be an ass," Mike muttered.

"Know what they call him around the station, honey? Hot Mike."

Sally had struggled to her feet, her cheeks burning. As she staggered against Mike, his arm went about her waist. Steadying her, he said, "Don't pay any attention to that knucklehead."

He felt a cold draft. The door behind them had opened. Without turning, he knew they were standing there, Eve and Harvey Terris.

Hazzard said, "This reminds me of a joke. There was this young couple, see, and they'd just been married a week, and—"

"That's enough," Mike said, his arm falling away from Sally.

"Oh, let Harry tell his little joke." Eve's voice was amused.

Hazzard grinned triumphantly. "Well, this couple had very modern ideas and—"

Mike spun on his heel and went to Eve. "We're going home. And we're giving Sally a lift. She's had a bit too much to drink."

Eve said, "It's getting late and I guess we really should go. But it doesn't appear that Sally plans to go with us."

He turned. Sally, clinging to Bruce Stockton's arm, was obviously on her way—elsewhere.

CHAPTER EIGHT

SALLY KAYE had decided to move. The other girls with whom she shared a three-room apartment-hotel suite were being altogether too kind, too understanding. She couldn't take it. She simply had to get away by herself, rebuild her life.

And so, taking a few hours off, she wandered through the canyons of the city. Downtown apartments, she quickly learned, were at a premium. They told her at a real estate office that she would have to consider a place considerably removed from the downtown area.

"But, that wouldn't do for me at all. There are times when I'm at the station until one o'clock in the morning."

The young man behind the desk looked thoughtful for a second. "Would you be willing to pay about twenty dollars more?"

She hesitated briefly. "Well, if I really had to, I suppose the answer is yes."

"We just listed this one. We won't have it long. An excellent address, one of the finest buildings in town. All de luxe five-room apartments."

"You can stop right there. It does sound like a terrific bargain, but I certainly don't want five rooms."

"You didn't let me finish. This is a two-room, the only one in the building. It was designed originally for the manager's quarters, but managers are getting particular these days."

The apartment was really charming, Sally thought. "It seems to be just what I had in mind," she told the pleasant, gray-haired woman who was the manager.

"You would be alone?" The woman asked the question a bit apologetically, as if hoping to cause no offense.

"Quite alone. I can give you references. Or, if it would expedite things, you could call the radio station where I work."

"Oh? So, you're in radio too? I wonder if you know Mr. Harvey Terris. His apartment is on this same floor."

"I know Mr. Terris," Sally said. She glanced about. The place was exactly what she wanted, but she didn't want to be running into people she knew. That was why she was leaving the guest house. She was seeking a sanctuary where she would be unknown and unpitied. It was bad enough having to face her fellow-workers at the station every day.

"When would you like to move in, Miss Kaye?"

"I—" Sally bit her lips. "I don't believe I'm going to be able to take it, after all. The more I think about the rent...." Her words trailed off and she moved toward the door. Opening it, she said, "Thank you so much for giving me your time."

"Don't mention it, Miss Kaye. But, think it over some more. You won't do any better than this, and frankly, I'd like a single business-girl like you."

Sally wasn't listening. She had caught sight of a girl hurrying down the corridor; there was something unmistakably furtive about her manner.

It was Eve Tremaine.

Leaving the building, Sally walked back to the station, apartment-hunting over for the day. It was back to the typewriter, back to the business of grinding out more publicity, thinking up more angles.

There was that story on Tony Ransford she had to get out. But she couldn't seem to keep her mind on it. She kept thinking about the hurrying figure in the corridor. Eve—hastening to keep a rendezvous with Harvey Terris.

Why be like that, she chided herself. There may have been a cocktail party in progress. But, two-thirty was much too early for a cocktail party, wasn't it?

Maybe, though, Eve was calling on Terris for strictly business reasons. Still, if that were the case, why that furtive air about her? Anyway, if it were business, why couldn't she discuss it with him at his office?

Sally was conscious of a rising excitement. Her pace quickened. She would walk into Mike's office. "Eve is in Terris' apartment, Mike." He would rush over there and his flimsy little dream house would come crashing down.

Then he'd come back to me. He would, he would—

The typewriter was clattering violently when she entered his office. "Mike," she said, breathlessly.

He continued to pound the keys with a sort of feverish fury. "Yeah, that does it!" Then, looking up, his fingers fell away from the machine. "Oh, it's you, Sally." His lean features relaxed in a welcoming smile. "Just the gal I want to see. I've got something here I want you to look over. I think it's good. The gizmo I'm using to bring around the dénouement is a nifty."

"Another television script?"

"Yes. I'm really pounding them out, nowadays. Did I tell you I finally finished those two I had laying around? Ted peddled them for me in Hollywood."

"He sold them? Why, that's marvelous, Mike!"

"He phoned me last night. Got me seven hundred and fifty bucks each." His gray eyes were shining. "Well, that's what marriage does for a man. Now that I've settled down, I'm getting things done. You know, I've had only one hangover since I've been a husband. And that was the morning after Manny's party." He paused.

She thought that the memory of that night was crossing his mind, that he was thinking of Bruce Stockton, wondering how far she had gone with the man.

But he wasn't thinking of Sally Kaye at all. He was thinking only of—success:

"Ted says if I keep turning stuff out, I'm bound to hit the top. And I will, Sally! Y'see, I've finally grown up. I'm on my way to making something of myself."

" 'Man's love is of man's life a thing apart,' " she murmured.

"What was that, Sally?"

"I was just muttering to myself, Mike."

He had pulled a sheet of paper from his typewriter and was clamping it to the other pages he had already written. "It's in the rough, Sally. But I'd like to get your reaction on it at this stage." Then: "By the way, did you come by for any special reason? You haven't been dropping in lately."

"No special reason," she said, taking the manuscript from him. "I'll give you a report on this later."

Head bowed, she left him. *Whatever Eve might be, she was good for Mike. Why spoil Mike's dream?*

Mike glanced at the electric clock on the bookcase. Seven-thirty. Eve should have been home a couple of hours ago. He picked up the telephone and dialed the Continental Broadcasting Company. "Eve Tremaine there?"

"Just a moment," the operator said. There was a long silence. Then: "Miss Tremaine isn't here."

Mike frowned and went back to his typewriter. But he couldn't concentrate. He rose and walked to the window, staring out toward the bridge and at the small craft which dotted the bay. He looked at the view without appreciation. His dinner had consisted of a couple of highballs and he was more than a little provoked.

He didn't think he was being unreasonable about expecting Eve to prepare dinner once in a while. And this happened to be one of the few nights they would have been able to enjoy a meal together. Most of the time, the unusual hours exacted by broadcasting kept them apart.

Yet during the first few weeks of their married life, they had managed to have dinner together at home fairly frequently. That had been an important time in his life; that was when the old habits had been put aside and he had gone to the typewriter religiously, pounding away for two or three hours after Eve had gone to bed. He had never worked harder. He was drinking very little and the eternal woman-chasing was in the past. Of course, there'd been times when he was beset by a devilish, itching restlessness, but the awareness of what he was accomplishing seemed to have a kind of sedative effect.

He looked at the half-completed script on his desk. He ought to get back to it. "It's amazingly good, Mike." That's what Sally had said about it ten days ago. "But I do think it should be smoothed up and a little more fully developed around the climax."

Ted O'Neill had made another point in his letter: "Expand it, Mike. I showed it to a story editor who's looking for an hour show. He said that this *Champagne and Orchids* of yours is right up his alley. So get working on it, Mike."

Mike lit a cigarette and began pacing up and down. Night before last, Eve had said, "Sorry, darling, I really intended to be home on time, but some of us went out for a drink after the program and you know how time flies."

"Who were 'some of us?' " he had asked carelessly.

"Oh, Harvey and a couple of the producers. We had dinner and—" She yawned. "I'm all in. Dead!" She had gone to their bedroom and, twenty minutes later, had been sound asleep.

He hadn't liked it. It was occurring altogether too often. But, he had said nothing. Eve could take care of herself. Had she a more passionate nature, he might have worried about her being always in the company of a man like Harvey Terris. But she had never warmed; she was as unresponsive now as she had been the first night of their honeymoon. She still lay quiet and relaxed in his arms—uncomplaining. She was, at least, a dutiful wife.

He crushed out his cigarette viciously. He wanted her right now. Wanted her terribly. He knew that it would be the same thing all over again, the vain effort to bring forth the desire, the abandon which he knew must lurk somewhere within her and finally, the conjuring up in his mind of erotic images from the past. Damn it, he was a man.

It was quarter of eight. He knew she wasn't broadcasting or rehearsing. What would she say when she came in? That Terris had asked her out for a drink and, for policy's sake, she had gone? Policy's sake, hell! Continental was making money on her voice. That should be enough. Why should that blasted, lecherous Terris—and the man was lecherous; there'd been more than a little talk—be seen so often in her company?

Not that Eve would be granting any physical favors. He knew her well enough to count on that. But that didn't prevent Terris from trying, did it?

"I have to be nice to him, Mike. He can make me or break me."

He'll make you, all right, if he can. Go ahead. Go and sleep with the sonofabitch. Sure, he can push you along. Don't depend on your talent. Make sure you'll be a top-notcher—and in a hurry, too. Don't lose any time. Just take it lying down.

Mike flung himself into the deep chair by the fireplace. What's the matter with me tonight? Eve's a good kid. Decent. She wouldn't go that far, no matter what the prize is. She has too much sense. She knows she's got what it takes. She's no mediocre number like that redhead, Lola, who has to play house with the boys. Eve has only to smile and be pleasant—and sing.

The telephone jangled.

"Mike—" It was Eve. "I won't be home for quite a little while."

"Listen, Eve—"

"This is important, Mike. Harvey is taking me over to meet Carrol Black. He's just flown in from Hollywood. You know who he is, don't you? He's with Wellington and Grant, one of the biggest advertising agencies on the coast."

"I know."

"Well, one of their clients is planning to put on a televison spectacular this fall and they are looking for a singer. Harvey says—"

"I don't care what Harvey says. You're coming right home. And now! There's a limit … "

She had hung up. Mike slammed down the receiver. What the hell had he bought, anyway? The way she'd hung up on him as if he were some persistent idiot trying to make a date! He was married to her and a husband had some rights, didn't he? He swung into the kitchen and poured a stiff drink.

The more he drank, the angrier he became. At ten o'clock, he slipped into his overcoat and walked out. He didn't know where he was going and he didn't care.

He descended the steep grade down Telegraph Hill to the valley below which was North Beach. Ordinarily, Mike would have walked slowly through the Italian quarter, relishing the spicy odors, looking into the colorful markets.

He didn't pause as he usually did on the corner where Grant, Broadway, and Columbus converge at crazy angles, and muse about the way two worlds met—Southern Europe and the Orient. He went straight on, crossing Grant Avenue, stepping into the Far East. It was Shanghai, Hong Kong, Canton, as they'd been in happier days.

China begins abruptly where Grant Avenue touches Broadway and Columbus. Twenty-five steps from one sidewalk to another. From Naples to Shanghai.

Tonight, Mike was hardly aware of these two worlds which had always intrigued his imagination. He plunged across Broadway into Chinatown, not slowing until he came to California Street.

There he stopped abruptly and looked up at Nob Hill and the bright lights of the great hotel. Bitter thoughts ricocheted in his mind. Carrol Black. Probably had a suite up there at the Mark. Usually stayed there. By now, the party was getting well under way. He could envision it readily enough. Scotch. Lots of good scotch flanked with buckets of ice and sweating siphons of soda. And Black—the big fat slob—loftily accepting homage, knowing how important he was. Black, looking over the women. Looking at Eve, mentally cupping her full breasts with his hands, undressing her with his eyes.

And Eve, standing there in all her innocence.

Damn it, he was going up there and find her, bring her home. She'd be furious with him. Perhaps she'd cry, "Mike! Humiliating me like that!"

And, it would be a humiliation for her. It would be as though he were telling the world he didn't trust her. He did trust her, didn't he?

Mike let go a deep breath. He turned and began retracing his steps. He was beating a retreat to Izzy's.

A girl sidled close to him, smiled invitingly and murmured a few words. She was young. He pushed past her. That was all the poor little thing had. Youth. She didn't have beauty, intelligence, and a singing voice the world wanted to hear.

He turned one last corner and there was Izzy's place. He clambered up the stairway, wedged through the crowd and found an empty spot at the end of the bar.

"How you, boy?" Izzy grinned.

Mike felt better already. Izzy always gave away the first drink even if he didn't know it. It wasn't in a glass but in his smile.

Mike ordered his alcohol and, looking around, saw nobody he knew. Well, within an hour or so, the crowd from the station would be drifting in. In the meantime, he decided, he would concentrate on his drinking. He'd finished three scotches when: "Hello, Mike darling!"

"Mary Sweet!" He greeted her warmly, glad that he had someone to talk to. "Who are you with, tonight? Bring him around and I'll buy him a drink."

"I'm on my own tonight, Mike."

He laughed. "Mary Sweet without a gentleman friend? Can't believe it."

"Mike Carlyle without a girl, who'd ever believe that! I think it must be fate, our running into each other on a night like this."

They took their drinks to a nearby table. For a brief spell, Mary's chatter was amusing, but, a couple of rounds later, he found himself slumping down in his chair, aware of her voice but not her words.

Staring into his glass, he seemed to be seeing Eve, her large blue eyes shining, her full soft lips curving in a winsome smile. And then, the picture faded and it was Sally that he saw.

If only Sally would come in. They would talk about—everything. The way they had talked in the past. Why couldn't they be friends? Why couldn't it be as it had been—her quick mind stimulating his and... She'd been right, though; they couldn't be just friends again after having been lovers. God, how he wanted her right now—

No. It was his wife he wanted. Eve. Again, he could see her fair, perfect features before his eyes—

"Mike!" Mary's fingers curved about his wrist.

He sat up straighter. The faces were gone, but—desire remained. Itching desire, tingling blood.

Mary. She was a lovely thing. Why hadn't he ever realized it before? Her body was softly round and—

He took her hands in his and pulled her closer to him, drew her onto his lap. He didn't see heads turn their way; he didn't see the grins. If Mary saw, she didn't care. Her warm, moist lips responded to his.

His hands strayed over her body. He wasn't thinking of where he was; he was thinking only that she was a woman—and desirable.

He though he heard a familiar voice. Hank Walton's? Oh, the hell with it. Then, he felt a hand on his shoulder.

"Mike, boy—" It was Izzy.

Mike looked up into the dark, disapproving face. The hell with Izzy.

"Mike, you act like this and you no stay here."

"Mary," Mike said breathing fast, "let's be on our merry way. We'll get a cab."

She stood up. "All right, Mike." Her smile was a promise.

He grinned at her crookedly. This was a woman, all right. He marveled at the loveliness he had never noticed before, at his own crazy and sudden need of her.

Fondling her in the cab, his passion mounted. How eagerly she was responding to him. "Lord," he breathed, his exploratory fingers trembling.

Once inside her apartment, they clung to each other fiercely. "Mike, I've been crazy about you for ages."

"Baby," he whispered, "I'm going to undress you and—" His hands lingered on her quivering flesh until finally he could bear it no longer. His body crushed against hers and he tortured himself with suspended ecstasy. Hours of ecstasy—shameless and abandoned—until, finally, the months-long, pent-up passion climaxed and left him sobbing with relief.

CHAPTER NINE

MARY SWEET was sleeping when he left a little before six-thirty that morning. He had looked down at her tangled hair, had seen the dark shadows under her eyes. Her creamy skin was paler than he had ever seen it before. She lay there, hardly breathing—utterly exhausted.

He smiled down at her. He, too, felt thoroughly spent, but it was a pleasant feeling. The unnerving tension which had been bothering him for weeks was completely gone.

Quietly, he closed the door behind him and, leaving the apartment, hailed an early cab. He was due at the studio at nine. Plenty of time for a shower and coffee, but not enough time for a scene.

He wondered if Eve would be awake and, if so, what she would say.

He frowned, nagged by a rising sense of guilt. Still, he told himself, didn't Eve go out and parade her body, inferring by every smile and gesture that she could be had—for a price? Wasn't that far more immoral than yielding to honest desire as he and Mary had done?

Mary was honest. She was the victim of her passions, but at least she made no demands. There were plenty of married women who were a lot less decent than Mary. Women who had not married because of love, but solely because of material considerations; women who submitted to a man only because it meant that they would be taken care of financially.

"Yes," Sally had once said, "there are women like that. Poor things who function out of avarice or fear rather than love. Centuries of oppression, centuries of having to accept a lord and master, have created a tradition some women still live by—driving a hard bargain. They don't realize they are living in a brave new world. They're victims of atavism."

It seemed that he could hear her soft voice beside him in the cab. He stirred uneasily, remembering. Remembering that when he had been unfaithful to Sally he had always hated himself afterward.

The weariness which had been so pleasant just a few minutes before was now a feeling of sick let-down. There was no reason for that guilty sensation. No point trying to analyze it. *Get your mind off it. You've a day's work ahead of you.*

There was a Betty and Benny script to write. Nice clean stuff that wasn't true to life at all. You'd never catch Benny sleeping with a woman other than his wife. Not Benny. For that matter, you wouldn't even catch him sleeping with his own wife. Not in a radio script you wouldn't.

Why, even if you took a ten-foot pole and touched reality only a little along the edges, the clubwomen, civic leaders, and churchmen would start breathing down your neck. Committees would call on the station manager and holler like hell: "You musn't tell people the truth. You'll give them bad ideas." Husbands might go out and sleep with strange females; women might sell themselves for fur coats and diamonds. It didn't matter that human beings did all this anyway.

Paying off the cab driver, Mike didn't notice right away the limousine in front of his apartment. Then he heard a deep voice:

"One more little kiss and we'll call it a night."

Mike turned.

They were standing in the doorway of the building, the fattish man and—Eve. They were close together, their lips meeting in a long kiss.

And then, the man was walking toward the limousine.

Carrol Black—and he's looking right at me without seeing me. It isn't as though he has forgotten having once met me, briefly. He's got Eve so much on his mind he's not even aware of his surroundings. I'm going to smash that smirk into his teeth.

At Carrol Black's approach, the chauffeur leaped out, flung open the car door and stood smartly at attention.

Mike was only a little more than twenty feet away but by the time he had covered the distance, the car door was shut. Black, crossing his eyes and leaning back, didn't notice the young man who reached out futilely for the door handle just as the limousine shot away.

Mike looked over his shoulder. Eve hadn't seen him. She was inserting the key in the lock.

Probably expecting to sneak in and find me asleep.

He was at her side just as she stepped into the foyer. "Hello, beautiful. Going somewhere?"

She turned with a startled expression on her face.

Wordlessly, he gripped her arm, led her to their apartment.

"Well?" he asked as they entered the living room.

"All right, I've been out," she said defiantly. "So what? What's wrong with that?"

"What's wrong with a married woman staying out with some man until dawn?" He laughed mirthlessly. "Am I supposed to consider that quite *au fait?*"

"See here, Mike, it just so happened that we sat around talking and it got later and later. That's all there is to it."

"Don't hand me that. I saw him slobbering all over you. God, haven't you any fastidiousness, Eve?"

She flared. "Look who's talking! Where have you been all night? You're just coming in. I can see that."

"Excellent strategy, darling. It's always good to take the offensive." Trying to make him feel guilty, was she? Well: "Let me tell you a few things." The words were rushing out. He was telling her what he thought of women who flaunted their bodies, who held out alluring bait, and: "Why don't you go ahead and actually sleep with the sonofabitch? Don't depend upon your talent alone. Make it a sure thing."

Suddenly, she spun away from him. Running toward the bedroom, she cried, shrilly. "I've had all of this I can stand!" She slammed the door shut. He heard the key turn in the lock.

The shower didn't do him much good. Neither did the aspirin and coffee. He fell asleep in a chair, awoke with a start an hour or so later. Feeling wretchedly depressed, he started off for the studio.

"Morning, Hazel," he muttered, passing the girl at the reception desk.

She shook a reproving finger at him. "Naughty, naughty!"

"What do you mean?" he asked dully.

"As if you didn't know." She giggled. "Izzy sure was sore, wasn't he?"

"Uh-huh," he mumbled absently, going on to his office. He had to turn out the Betty and Benny script. He sat down at his desk and began reading the preceding episode. Betty had been maneuvered into being a babysitter for the day and little Edgar with whom she was supposed to be sitting had got himself lost. Betty had searched everywhere, frantic with worry. She called Benny who came dashing home from his office. And thus the episode ended.

Mike scowled at the script. Did people actually listen to this disintegrating garbage? It was a wonder they didn't smell it long before it hit their loudspeakers.

In any event, whether they listened or not, he had to write it. If he didn't, Hubbard's Department Store would be very much provoked.

BETTY & BENNY
Episode No. 48
Aug. 25, 3.45-4.00 P.M.
Sponsor: Hubbard's

Theme Music (recording)

ANNOUNCER: And now, ladies and gentlemen, we bring you another episode in the lives of that lovable young couple, Betty and Benny. You will recall that in the previous episode, little Edgar Stine was lost. As today's exciting scene opens, Benny arrives home to help lock for Edgar.

(THEME MUSIC OUT)

BENNY: (Breathlessly) No sign of Edgar yet?

BETTY: (Sobbing) Oh, darling! I've searched everywhere.

BENNY: I don't see why you wanted to mind that old bat's little brat anyway.

Mike stared at the dialogue bleakly. What was he thinking of, putting in "old bat" and "little brat?" He knew, very well, that mothers who were old bats and who had brats wouldn't like it in the least. And they would write to the station and complain. And Hazzard would raise hell.

Mike ripped the sheet of paper out of the typewriter, crumpled it and tossed it into the wastebasket. He got up. A drink might help him find the lost darling.

Starting down the corridor, he hesitated. His eyes went to Sally's office. Involuntarily, he turned and went in.

"You don't look too good, Mike," she said.

"And I don't feel good, either. I'm fed up with this joint—"

"Temporary nausea, Mike. You really don't mean that. Probably when you woke up this morning—that is, if you went to sleep at all—you wished you were dead. Now you wish that you didn't have to work. You'll be all right tomorrow if you'll just take it easy in the grog department."

Mike grinned. It wasn't what she said, but the spirit in which she said it. He couldn't quite analyze her effect on him. It was intangible; something precious from within her that always reached him. The atoms which made up their beings, he reflected, must like each other and holler, "Hi, pal," when they came within hailing distance.

Sally's face had become very thoughtful. "They've been wanting you over at Continental, Mike. Hasn't it occurred to you it might be better over there? You and Eve would see more of each other."

"Maybe." Possibly Sally was right.

Mike found suddenly that he did not want the drink he had been on his way to get. He returned cheerfully to his office.

Mike ground out the Betty and Benny script in an hour. He wanted it off his mind before calling Terris. When it was finished, he passed it over to one of the stenographers for mimeographing. Then he went out to a drugstore and entered a phone booth.

He dialed the Continental Broadcasting Company's number and finally reached Terris.

"Hello, Carlyle." Terris' voice, Mike thought, seemed tempered with a certain wariness. "Well, what can I do for you?"

Mike returned evenly: "You can give me that job we were talking about a month or so ago."

There was a silence, then a soft cough. "What job was that?"

"The one you had on your mind the night of Manny Rhodes' party."

"Oh. Well, to be frank, things have changed since then. We brought in a man from the East and—"

"I see. I suppose I'll have to settle for a producer's job."

"I can't promise you a thing at the moment, Carlyle. Actually, we're overstaffed at the present time. Sorry, but you know how it goes. Drop by, though, sometime and say hello, won't you?"

Mike hung up. What the hell. He knew very well that the Continental net could always find a place for a good production man. They'd wanted him before. Why not now? He had not dreamed he'd get this reaction from Terris. There was some reason for it. But what? Well, it was no use speculating.

Mike rushed outside and into the bar across the street, irritated with himself for having called Terris. Three drinks in rapid succession didn't improve his mood. Why in hell had he given

Terris the chance to turn him down as if he were some punk kid looking for a first chance in broadcasting?

He consumed a hamburger, washed it down with a glass of milk, and became a bit more composed.

Back at his desk, he found a note from Harry Hazzard. "See me at once," the station manager had scrawled.

He stopped by a moment at Sally's office, showed her the message. "Know what's on his mind?"

She regarded him peculiarly. "I'm not sure, but I think it may be about your little fling last night. The station's buzzing, Mike."

"So that's it. Where'd you get it?" He remembered Hazel. She had been in Izzy's last night, but it wouldn't be like her to blurt out anything. "From Hank Walton?"

Sally nodded. "He's made quite a story of it."

Mike knew Hank's joking way of knifing someone. Hank wanted his job, had wanted it for a long time. Now Hank was probably closing in for the kill. It was a good sharp knife that Hank carried, one that was sheathed in a hearty guffaw.

"According to Hank—" Sally began.

"You talking about me?" Walton stood in the doorway, his long face wreathed in a wider than usual grin. He winked at Mike. "Hi, Casanova. What's the idea of grabbing off all the good-looking dames in the station? Why don't you give the rest of us a break?" He moved closer and, nudging Mike with his elbow, said in a confidential whisper, "That Mary's built, isn't she?" His eyes gleamed lasciviously.

Mike gave him a blank stare. "How should I know?" He swung away and went down the corridor to Hazzard's office.

As Mike entered, Hazzard said coldly, "Sit down, Carlyle."

Mike eased his long body into a chair. Somehow, the little station manager looked almost like a stranger. Mike wondered about that until he realized this was the first time he had ever seen those thin lips of Hazzard's held in a perfectly straight line.

"Carlyle," Hazzard began, "you don't seem to realize that a radio station is a public service and it's absolutely essential that our public behavior be above reproach." Harry paused for effect.

He frowned when Mike replied by lighting a cigarette.

"This is damned serious, Carlyle. Damned serious for you."

"Okay, Harry. But don't try to take me over your knee and spank me." Mike was in no mood for this.

Hazzard pounded his fist on the desk. "I don't like your attitude! What I have to say to you is for your own good. I don't ordinarily waste my time talking without good reason—"

Mike sensed the impending storm but, somehow, he didn't care. "Go ahead, Harry. Get up on your hind legs and bark, if it will make you feel better. I'll listen. I've got nothing else to do—except get out a half dozen scripts today. And, personally, I don't give a damn whether they get out or not."

"That's the trouble with you." Hazzard's voice rose to a shaky treble. "You don't give a damn for anything. You don't give a damn for the station. You're supposed to be a respectable married man, yet you go chasing around, getting thrown out of a bar because of licentious behavior with a tramp like Mary Sweet."

"It's none of your damned business, Harry."

"The hell it isn't!"

"And don't go calling Mary a tramp."

"Well, that's just what she is. If she didn't have a voice that goes over, she wouldn't be around here five minutes more. As soon as she comes in, I'm going to tell her that from here on out, she's going to have to watch her step. But good." Hazzard paused for breath. Then, leaning forward, he went on, "Listen, Carlyle, you're one of our executives. You're supposed to be a representative type. You can't chase around in public view."

"There are plenty of guys in this station who chase skirts like a bull chases a red flag."

Hazzard stood up, his face purpling with rage. "If you're referring to me—well, whatever I do, Carlyle, I don't do in public.

I don't chippy around bars. But if you think you can come in here and accuse me of anything, you're crazy as hell."

Hazzard had reached over and punched a button on his desk.

A stenographer poked in her head. "Yes, Mr. Hazzard?"

"Get Walton in here," he ordered.

Hank must have been standing outside the door for he came in almost immediately.

Hazzard had turned toward Mike. "Carlyle, you're—"

"I quit," Mike interrupted quietly.

There was a moment's silence. Mike grinned

"Beat you to it, didn't I, Harry? Well, I've known for quite some time that Hank's been after my job. He's been all over the studio, hacking away with his chisel."

"See here," Hank blustered, taking a step forward. But as Mike drew back his right arm, Hank hurriedly retreated, taking up a position next to Hazzard.

Mike smiled thinly, watching the fear grow in Harry's eyes. "I don't know why I don't knock your heads together." At the door he turned and looked back at Hank. "Take good care of Betty and Benny. And, listen, here's a nice, juicy piece of scandal for you." He lowered his voice to a stage whisper, "Betty and Benny aren't married at all. They're just living together—the nasty things."

Mike removed his personal belongings from his desk and then went to Sally's office. She wasn't there. Probably, out on her rounds, contacting the newspapers. So Mike got his pay from the cashier's office and quietly walked out of the station.

On his way home, he experienced a kind of lightheartedness. For the first time in more than a year, he didn't have to look forward to the drudgery of grinding out radio programs to meet broadcast deadlines. He could sleep as long as he wished tomorrow morning and he intended to. Tonight—tonight, he'd go out with Eve and they'd hit the night-spots together. He would dance as much as she wanted, and he'd be humorous and gay. She'd like that. All this morning's unpleasantness would be forgiven and forgotten.

He could see it now. The infernal, nerve-beating work at the station had been getting him down; it had soured him. And his sourness, his rotten disposition had caused the trouble between him and Eve. Well, he'd make it all up to her.

His eye was caught by the display in a liquor store window. He didn't need liquor. This exhilarating feeling of freedom was enough. But he succumbed to the classic desire to celebrate. This was a special occasion, wasn't it?

He entered the store and bought a bottle of twelve-year-old scotch. Then, with the packing tucked under his arm, he ran for a passing cable car.

He hurried up the stairs, flung open the door and called, "Eve?" He was certain she would be home. She had no programs today and, after having been up so late … "Eve!"

There was no answer. He went into the bedroom, thinking she might still be sleeping. Immediately, he noticed that all the things which usually cluttered up the vanity were gone. The closet door stood agape. He could see the closet was empty. Then he noticed the note on the pillow.

He unfolded it, looked at Eve's neat, backhanded writing:

Dear Mike: After what happened this morning, I think it would be best if we didn't see each other for a little while. I am flying south today. Have a chance to work out of Continental's Hollywood studios. Meantime, much love and thanks for everything you've done for me. In a few weeks, we can talk things over. Will write.

Eve

Mike, twisting the note between his fingers, went out to the kitchen. Then he slowly unwrapped the bottle of scotch, got out some ice, and made a highball.

There was no anger in him. No feeling at all. He was completely stunned.

Halfway through the bottle, he began to feel sorry for himself. Here he sat in an empty house—no wife, no job. No future, no nothing. Not even anyone to talk to.

He hardly was aware of it, but he was dialing the station's number. He was asking to speak to Miss Sally Kaye.

"Sally?"

"Oh, Mike! I just got back five minutes ago and—well, I know about it. I'm awfully sorry."

Her words soothed him. Unaccountably, he felt better. "What time will you be through?"

"I'm nearly finished now," she replied. "Why?"

"I want to see you. I need to talk to you, Sally. We'll have dinner at Izzy's—"

"No, Mike. I've told you."

"Eve has left me—for Hollywood." The way he said it made it appear that it was all over between him and Eve. It really wasn't. Her letter had made it clear this was to be only a temporary separation, hadn't it? But he wanted to talk with Sally.

Sally's voice trembled. "Eve's left you?" There was a pregnant silence. Then: "I'll be home in just about forty-five minutes, Mike. You can pick me up there. Oh, I don't think I've told you, but I've moved. I'm living on Pine Street now."

He wrote down her address.

CHAPTER TEN

Hardly five minutes after Sally had entered her little apartment, the buzzer rang.

Her heart went out to him as he came toward her, a contrived grin fastened on his lips. She could see that he had been drinking, but the droop to his shoulders and the hurt look in his eyes had not been caused by alcohol.

"Sit down, Mike. There's a drink in the kitchenette if you think you need another."

"I've really had enough. Well, maybe I could use just one more." Together they went out to the kitchen and, while Sally took the ice from the tray, he measured out the scotch.

Leaning back against the piled-up pillows on the studio couch, Mike said, "Nice place you have here."

She saw his features relax as he looked at the books he had given her, at the little graduated row of five imitation ivory elephants. He had bought them for her in a Grant Avenue shop one noisy and unbelievably happy night during the Chinese New Year celebration. They had laughingly named the first three Mike, Spike, and Ike, and the two little ones—because they couldn't think up any more rhymes—Chink and Dink.

For days after she had moved into the place, she had kept the books and all the others gifts packed away far back in the closet. But they'd been so much a part of her, she had brought them out. Hiding them hadn't eased her pain.

His head was resting on her shoulder. Tenderly she stroked his thick brown hair, smoothed his forehead. "You seem to be worn out, Mike."

He didn't say anything for a long moment. Then, "All I had for dinner last night were scotch highballs and, since then, I've been living on more scotch and a few cups of coffee. I think I'd feel better once I got one of Izzy's steaks inside me."

She laughed softly. How like the old days this was. This going down to Izzy's for a steak.

Arm in arm, they walked down Pine Street, turned the corner.

Then it was as though there'd never been any black hiatus. Why, it seemed as if it were only yesterday that they were following this very route and that Mike was giving her those intimate little sidewise glances, increasing the pressure of his fingers on her arm, now and then.

It was early when they walked into Izzy's. Much too early for the usual crowd who had to drink themselves into an eating mood. For Izzy's dinners were anything but pretentious. They lacked the glitter of polished silver, the snowy whiteness of fine linen, and the imposing unctuousness of perfect service. But these deficiencies were more than made up for by the fact that Izzy's steaks were gustatory delights.

Izzy was resting his bulk against the bar as Mike and Sally came in. His dark, cherubic face, which seemed too small for his enormous body, broke into a wide smile when he caught sight of Sally.

"Hallo," he called happily. "Where you been, Sally?" He darted an admonishing look toward Mike.

Mike felt his cheeks grow hot. He had a vague recollection of having pawed Mary. It must have been some performance to evoke a reaction like this from tolerant Izzy. Probably Hank Walton hadn't had to embroider his tale very much.

"Made an ass of myself last night, didn't I, Izzy?"

Izzy sighed. "I no understand. You good boy, but—" He gestured hopelessly. "What's eating you, Mike?"

"I wish I knew. Some day, maybe, I'll find out. In the meantime, we're having dinner, Izzy. Tell Joe to carve up a steer—"

They ordered highballs and Izzy drew a small beer for himself. But he had no chance to drink with them because a new customer vociferously demanded service.

Glancing toward the far end of the bar, Mike saw the pudgy little man who was making the racket. "That's Al Farrington," he told Sally. "A producer at Continental. Been there for six years, grinding out sustaining shows. He's a poor fish at the bottom of the tank."

"Maybe," Sally said softly, "he's trying to drink his way to the top." She broke off, catching the look in Mike's eyes, and hastily disarmed him with a smile. This was no night to preach; this was a night to live to the fullest. *Oh, darling, we'll go home together tonight, and you will hold me in your arms.*

"Izzy," Mike called after their second drink, "tell Joe we'll be in the last booth."

Hand in hand, they left the bar and walked to the table. Mike smiled down at the thick, savory soup. "I think I'm going to live now." A few moments later: "That would be a meal in itself for anybody except a starving man." He leaned back with a sigh.

"What are your plans, Mike? Or have you made any?"

"I'm going to pull out of San Francisco. All the big television shows emanate from either Hollywood or New York."

"But you're not going to New York." There were peculiar overtones in her voice.

"No. Hollywood's my best bet. Ted O'Neill's down there."

"And so is Eve. Mike, be honest with me!" Her eyes pleaded. "Do you still love her?"

He didn't want to answer. And, fortunately, he didn't have to. Joe—Izzy's one-man culinary department, doubling as waiter—was leaning into the booth, placing the sizzling two-inch-thick steaks on the table. Then he set down a large plate of crisp, fried potatoes.

"Lord, Sally! I'm starved!"

She smiled sadly.

They had just finished dinner and were about to leave when they heard a familiar voice: "Izzy, my good man, pour out the best. This is a night for celebration. Behold the new program manager—"

"Our good friend, Hank," Mike muttered.

Hank Walton, seeing them come out of the booth, staggered toward them. "Hi." He held out his hand. "No hard feelings over my getting your job?"

Mike ignored the outstretched hand. "Someone had to get it."

"That's the spirit," Hank said, beaming. "Have a little drink on it. Izzy, we're having a drink on it."

Izzy leaned over the bar. "You get a new job, eh?"

"Sure thing," Hank said loudly. "Got Mike's job today."

A pained expression came over Izzy's face. "That right, Mike?"

"Correct."

"Say, that not so good. You get another job, Mike?"

"Not yet, Izzy. But I will."

"Sure you will. You good boy." He turned to mix the drinks.

Hank said, "We're all good friends, huh?" He sought to put his arm around Sally.

Sally edged away.

His drink finished, Mike said, "Let's be on our way, Sally."

She assented eagerly. She was anxious to leave. She'd sensed his increasing tension.

"One more drink," Hank insisted, grabbing Mike's arm.

"No. No more." Mike jerked his arm loose.

Hank bared his yellow teeth. "You're sore because I got your job."

Sally said, "Don't be like that, Hank." She'd seen the hard glitter in Mike's eyes. If Hank wasn't careful—

Hank wasn't careful. "Too good to drink with me, are you? But you're not so good you can hang onto your job, you two-timing drunk. That's what you are. Marry the swellest little girl in the studio and then go out and sleep with every tramp you can pick up." Hank's long resentment had reached a peak. He picked up someone's glass of beer and threw it—glass and all—into Mike's face. "Have a drink on me, you bum."

Mike jerked free of Sally's grasp. He drew his right hand back, then it flashed up and forward. There was a sharp, crunchy sound. Hank went over backward and crashed to the floor, his head resting in a spittoon. Slowly, his hand went to his shattered nose.

On the street, Mike said, "I've been wanting to let him have it for a year. And, when he asked for it—" His laughter rang out. "I feel swell. Don't know whether it was poking Walton in the puss, or whether it was the meal, but—"

He looked down at her, his eyes gleaming. "Sally—it's been a long time, hasn't it?"

The words hovered on her lips: *You've got to tell me first. Is it all over between you and Eve?* Then, suddenly, she didn't care. Just to be with him once again—that would be enough.

He was helping her into a cab, giving the driver the address of her apartment. She leaned back in his arms, shuddering with delight when his warm lips caressed the hollow of her throat.

"Mike."

"H'm?"

"I'll call the station in the morning. Tell them I won't be in until late."

"You're taking the whole day off, baby."

Was it four days—or five—since Eve had left? Mike sat on the edge of his bed, holding his head in his hands. He'd drunk too much last night after he had quarreled with Sally.

She had said quietly, "I thought that, just so long as I had you, it would be enough. But, I'm beginning to realize I haven't got you. There'll always be Eve."

"But I'm not with Eve. I'm with you, aren't I?"

"For now."

"Isn't now enough?"

"No, Mike."

He had laughed. Had pushed her down on the studio couch, had pulled up her skirts.

"No!" She'd meant it, too. He hadn't realized that, at first. Titillated by her furious writhing, he'd begun to have his way with her when suddenly she had freed herself, had stood up, panting.

"I told you no!"

"Why, you little—" He'd said nasty things, things he hadn't meant, during that rage which stemmed from frustrated passion.

Sally had cried, her face white, "Get out!"

And he had left, had made for the nearest bar, had drunk until the two o'clock closing time.

There was something else. Gradually, it started coming back to him. He'd phoned someone from the bar.

He'd called Hollywood, had talked with Ted O'Neill. "I'm coming south, Ted. Just as soon as I can sub-let the apartment." And Ted had said, "Fine, boy. Wire me when you leave and I'll be on hand to meet you."

Thanks to the housing shortage in San Francisco, Mike had no difficulty finding a tenant for the Telegraph Hill apartment. The rented grand piano was taken away, his cartons of personal belongings were carried off by the men from a storage company.

He stood in the living room, glancing about, his eyes lingering on the desk where he had worked those first weeks. For a little while, life had been so good. That business of settling down with a wife, coming home evenings to write creatively ...

He walked to the desk and, opening a drawer, pulled out the checkbook. The figures showed a balance of $973.44. It was a joint account but it was unlikely that Eve had drawn many checks against it. She had her own salary.

But—he'd better make sure. There may have been some household expenses and Eve might have written a check for fifty or sixty dollars. Perhaps, even a hundred. He picked up the phone and called the bank.

"Yes, Mr. Carlyle. I'll look up your account. One moment, please." The bank clerk spoke in crisp tones. While Mike waited, he wondered if all bank clerks spoke so crisply to suggest crisp banknotes.

The clerk's voice cut in: "Your balance shows one hundred and forty-two dollars and eighty-three cents—"

"What?" Mike gasped. "Are you sure?"

"I have your file in front of me."

"Thanks," Mike mumbled and cradled the phone.

He thought of his car. He'd have to sell it. That would give him a few hundred, anyway.

CHAPTER ELEVEN

STEPPING DOWN from the plane, Mike saw Ted O'Neill among the group that was waiting.

"What happened, Mike?" Ted asked as they started off together. "Did the station give you another vacation?"

"Yeah. A permanent one." Mike grinned. "Tell you about it later."

"Okay. Now, let's see about your baggage. We'll get it in my car and strike out for my place."

Mike pointed to his suitcase. "This is all I have. Shipped down the rest of my stuff by express."

"You're staying with me, of course."

Mike nodded. With Ted, one didn't make polite sounds like: "If you're sure I'm not putting you out."

Ted stopped to buy a fifth, and then drove on to his place in Sunset Boulevard.

Looking at the impressive building, Mike said, "Times must be prosperous, Ted."

"I'm getting along." Ted chuckled, leading the way through the somewhat ornate lobby. "Real fancy joint, isn't it? Nice thing about it, it's just as comfortable as it is fancy."

Mike thought, as he sprawled in an easy chair, that it did look comfortable—and expensive. Glancing toward the hallway, he called, "Need any help out there, Ted?"

Ted's voice came from the kitchen: "Relax, boy. I'll have these drinks built in nothing flat."

A few minutes later, Ted returned with the tall glasses, placing them on the table between the two chairs. Mike took one and lifted it to his lips. "That helps." Then: "Seems like things are going all right with you."

Ted grinned. "Well, I've never made so much money in my life, but on the other hand—well, leave us not talk about my ulcers. Leave us talk about you. Just what happened up there in Frisco. Did you up and quit?"

"I beat Harry Hazzard to the draw. By about two seconds."

"Who got your job?"

"Hank Walton."

Ted shook his head. "Well, that just goes to show it doesn't take brains to be a success in radio. The chief requirement seems to be a big mouth. Supplement that with a sharp chisel and, automatically, you're an executive. Why, that cretin couldn't write a note to the milkman."

"You worked with Walton once, didn't you?"

"Around him," Ted said, a reminiscent light in his eyes. "At a little station out in Beverly Hills. I was handling the publicity for 'em. Anyway, Hank chiseled in as a salesman, gouged his way into an announcer's job, and eventually weaseled his way to the manager's desk. The owners thought they had a boy wonder until—"

And so, he and Ted talked and drank. Ted must have known about the separation from Eve but he didn't bring it up.

Finally, Mike said. "Eve walked out on me—and not without reason, either."

Ted's blue eyes flickered. Then he looked down into his drink. "H'm," he said noncommittally.

"She said we ought to remain apart for a little while. Said she'd write me, but I haven't heard from her yet. Know how she's making out?"

"That's my business, boy. As of last week, I've been head of public relations for Continental's television department. Yeah, she's making out okay. I caught her first TV appearance last night. She was rung in at the last minute, substituting for a nice little gal who'd been waiting months for this chance. But the little gal had come down with a bad case of flu, according to the press releases." Ted's pleasantly homely face had become very serious. "Mike."

"Yes?"

"Oh, skip it. Let's get down to business. First of all, have you finished that hour script?"

"You mean *Champagne and Orchids?*" Mike sighed. "I haven't been able to get back into the mood, Ted. Damn it, with one thing and another—"

"You could latch onto one of these fifteen hundred dollar a week writing jobs if it weren't for your penchant for getting into trouble. I mean that, Mike. You've got the stuff. You could've moved up to one of the big webs, months ago. But you kind of liked being where you were, the big frog in a small puddle, able to take time off for one thing and another."

There was a long silence. Then Ted went out and refilled the glasses. When he returned, Mike said, "I'm not saying you're one hundred per cent right. But, anyway, I'm out of the puddle. I'm ready to get my teeth into something. As a matter of fact, I have to if I expect to get said teeth to crunch t-bones—"

Ted O'Neill put his head over to one side. "With the money you and Eve were making and that twelve hundred you got for those scripts not so very long ago—aw, it's none of my business. How much do you figure you need, Mike?"

"Thanks. But, I'll be able to get by, for a while anyway."

"Kind of glad you're none too flush, boy. This way, you won't be pulling out for a hotel in a hurry. I like having you around, even if you are a bad influence."

"Bad influence?"

"Hell, yes. Here I am guzzling grog again and for weeks, up until tonight, I was sticking strictly to benzedrine."

In the morning, they drank tomato juice and coffee. Ted groaned, "I feel like someone sawed the top off my conk, shoved in a crew of riveters, and then nailed it back on with spikes." But, he managed a grin, and there was a spark in his eyes which, gleaming through the red blotches, made his eyeballs look like highgrade agates.

After Ted had left, Mike telephoned Continental. He asked for Eve.

"Miss Tremaine is not here right now. Whom shall I say called?"

"What's her home phone number?"

"Sorry, sir, but we cannot give out that information."

"I'm her husband, Michael Carlyle. Just flew in from San Francisco and I want to locate her."

"One moment, please." Then, after a long pause, "Miss Tremaine is staying at the La Playa."

It wasn't quite nine-thirty when Mike entered the impressive lobby of the hotel and went to the desk.

"Mrs. Carlyle?" The clerk looked through his files. "Sorry, but there's no Mrs. Carlyle registered."

"She may've registered under the name of Eve Tremaine—"

"Oh, Miss Tremaine." The man nodded. "She checked out yesterday. My impression was that she was leaving the city."

"She left a forwarding address?"

"No, sir."

Mike strode from the lobby into the cocktail lounge where he ordered a highball. Could Eve have returned to San Francisco repentant, hoping for a reconciliation? Lord, what would the poor kid think, walking into their apartment and finding it occupied by strangers? And then, calling the station, only to find that he wasn't there. She'd ask them if they knew where he had gone. But he hadn't told anybody.

Finishing his drink, he hurried to the telegraph desk in the lobby. He sent her a wire, care of Continental in San Francisco ... *and please get in touch with me immediately. Am staying with Ted O'Neill.*

On his way back to Ted's, Mike bought a six-pack of beer, some cheese and French bread. While waiting for an answer to his wire, he thumbed through the telephone directory and began to map out a systematic job-hunting campaign. If he and Eve were going to get back together, and it looked as though they were, he'd have to line up a job immediately.

With a berth at some radio station, he'd have enough time to do some writing. Then, with a few sales to his credit, he might land one of those fat jobs that Ted talked about.

From the telephone directory, he copied down a complete list of radio stations—and graded them according to their importance, making but one exception—Continental.

He picked up the phone and began calling. A while later he was reflecting that he seemed to have chosen a bad day for job-hunting. No one seemed to be in. But, finally, the manager of a small station said, "Drop over tomorrow morning, Carlyle. I might have something for you."

He was still dialing when Ted arrived at three-thirty.

"Ah, beer! Just what I've been craving, Mike." He opened a bottle and thrust a hunk of cheese between two thick slices of bread. "Making a date, boy?" he asked between mouthfuls.

"Trying to line up a job. This guy in North Hollywood told me there might be an opening. Name's Powers."

Ted munched and looked thoughtful as Mike went on talking. Then:

"See here, Mike, you can do a helluva lot better than that. That's a chiseling little outfit. Patent Medicine Powers has almost had his license canceled by the Commission."

"That's beside the point. I want a job, something that will get me over the hump until I finish *Champagne and Orchids* and whip up a couple of other scripts. I'm ready to settle down,

Ted. Honest. I'm going to patch things up with Eve, and—" He frowned. "What's the matter, Ted?"

Ted turned away from him and went across the room. For a moment or so he stared out the window. Then he said, "Mike—" Then he stopped and didn't say anything. He came back to where Mike stood.

"I guess you'd better look at today's *Spotlight*." Ted pulled a copy of the radio, television and film trade paper from his pocket. "It's on the second page."

Mike took the paper and read:

RADIO WARBLER RENO-BOUND

Eve Tremaine, Continental's newest discovery, left today for Reno to get a divorce from her husband, Michael Carlyle, former production chief for a San Francisco broadcasting station.

Staring at the printed words, Mike muttered, "I'll be damned."

Glancing up at the garish façade of the building he was leaving, Mike pondered the curious magnificence of Hollywood. Structures housing prosaic industries were splashed with blatant colors. There was the conflicting architecture of a dozen countries and as many eras. A miniature palace, set like a jewel in the center of a lush garden spot was a thing of beauty except for the tremendous whirling sign on its roof which proclaimed: *Jumbo Hamburgers.*

Everything was fancy in this town, including the brush-off. These suave, enthusiastic executives had made an art of it. "Thanks so much for dropping in, Mr. Carlyle. Be sure and keep in touch with me, won't you? Call me Thursday." And on Thursday, "Call me Monday." And so on. They kept their victims bouncing in the air like jugglers' balls. Why, Mike wondered, why couldn't they come right out and say, "Nothing doing.

Y'know this is a glamour business and everybody wants in, so there's no labor shortage with us."

He had been skipping around the vast area which was Los Angeles since early that morning. The technique hadn't varied and he didn't believe it would be any different at the next station on his list. He thought he might just as well go back to Ted's and call Patent Medicine Powers, tell the little pipsqueak he'd take that stinking job.

Then a thought occurred to him. Why not try Continental again, after all? He knew Baldwin. Walt Baldwin had drunk Mike's liquor and had obtained satisfactory results from Mike's address book. Mike would have preferred to get a position from a stranger, but these strangers in Hollywood were entirely too strange.

The receptionist behind the desk in the Continental foyer was chatting with a sleek young man in pastel blue slacks and a darker blue polo shirt open at the throat. The girl was punctuating most of her sentences with admiring little laughs, proving that polo shirt had an important post.

Mike walked up to the desk and stood waiting. The girl, whose yellow hair was ringed in shining, tight curls, was saying, "It was simply out of this world, Mr. Sloss. Especially the pay-off gag. I've never heard anything funnier."

The young man admitted it was damned good. Then, he let out a long sigh. "Look, honey, what I stopped by for was to tell you our date's off for tonight. The wife's roped me in on a dinner party."

"Oh!" she exclaimed and the disappointment showed in both her voice and face. "I wish I'd known sooner. I turned down a date with my steady."

Sloss pinched her chin. "You've no right to have a steady boy friend. You ought to be kept in circulation."

Mike had had enough. He moved closer to the desk, easing Sloss to one side. The girl looked at him coldly.

"I want to see Mr. Baldwin," Mike told her.

"Who's calling please?"

"Mike Carlyle."

She murmured into the phone: "Mr. Carlyle to see Mr. Baldwin." Then: "You can go right in, Mr. Carlyle." Her manner had thawed visibly. She gave him a smiling, sidelong glance. "It's the first door to the left."

Walt Baldwin pumped Mike's hand. "Welcome to Hollywood, Mike. It's swell, seeing you again. What brings you south?"

Mike sat down. "I resigned from my job in San Francisco. Thought I'd see what Hollywood has to offer."

"Oh." Baldwin's voice covered a wide range in that one syllable. His expression changed subtly. He looked at Mike as though he were gazing down from the heights. The genial smile was replaced by a frown.

"Excellent idea," he said slowly. "Plenty of opportunities down here. No doubt," and he looked hopeful, "you've lined something up already?"

"Not exactly," Mike said.

"I see. I see." Baldwin glanced at his wristwatch. "Well, can you tie that? I told the wife I'd be home early to drive her to this damned cocktail party and—"

Mike interrupted, a bit sharply. "I figure I could fit in here at Continental quite nicely."

"No doubt about that, Carlyle. But we're over-staffed, right now. Nothing I'd like better than to have you with us." He pushed back his chair and rose briskly. "I've got to shove along, now. But, you be sure to keep in touch with me, won't you? Why don't you call me next week? Say—Monday. That's it, Monday!" he exclaimed as if inspired. "Now, be sure to get in touch with me Monday."

Mike, passing by the information desk on his way out, looked at the blonde with mild interest.

She was smiling at him, her eyes provocative. She fluttered her long eyelashes and put down the powder puff and small mirror she had been holding.

He hesitated. He had been putting in a couple of hours every night on *Champagne and Orchids;* another few nights and he'd be finished. "Sure," Ted had said, "it's a gamble. You're slanting it for this one market but, if you bring it off, you won't have any financial worries for a while. You can get going on other stuff."

Mike thrust his hands deep into his pockets. He really should be making tracks for Ted's place. Still it would be nice to have a cocktail. And, it would be nice to have company, too. He said to the little blonde, "Getting ready to leave?"

"Uh huh."

"I suppose you're going straight home to read a good book?"

"I guess I'll have to."

"Oh, you don't really have to. You could have a cocktail with me."

And before Mike knew it, the evening and half the night were gone.

He had started out to have a drink or two with a blonde. And, here he was, sitting in a smoky night club, the fifth in a zig zag jaunt around Hollywood.

He looked at the girl who sat opposite him. Her cheeks were flushed and her eyes sparkled. She was enjoying every second of it. It seemed to be mighty big stuff to her, this rubbing elbows with celebrities.

Cute little youngster, he reflected. Too bad she didn't pay more attention to her hair. It was awfully dark at the roots. Almost black. He didn't like to look at it. Well, he didn't have to. He could look at her piquantly pointed breasts.

"Having fun, Mitzi?" he asked.

"It's been swell, Mike. And, gosh, you're the grandest dancer!"

"Well, it's getting late, Mitzi. One more dance and—" His hand reached out and covered hers. It was a tiny, hot hand. He wondered if her body were as hot. But, hell. Why did he have to go and start getting ideas like that? The kid couldn't be more than seventeen.

"Okay, Mike, one more dance."

He didn't hold her too close, but her body pressed against his invitingly. A bit surprised, he looked down at her. Their eyes met. Deliberately, he lowered his hand and drew her hips close to his. She pressed even closer. The tips of her fingers burned on his neck.

Assured, Mike said bluntly, "Shall we go somewhere less public?"

"I live alone," she replied.

They danced back toward their table. It seemed to him that there had been something crudely calculated about those movements of hers which had induced desire in him. But, searching her face, he saw only demureness. Did she know what she had done? Did she know what she was letting herself in for? Maybe this little dumb bunny figured that he wanted to take her home for just a little necking.

"I'm going to do things to you, Mitzi," he said softly. "I'm going to make you live."

She looked up at him, her lips parted in a little smile.

His throat felt tight. He remembered the way she had looked at him in the foyer at Continental. Maybe there had been an instantaneous attraction—that quick spark which, bursting into flames, burns down the inhibitory barriers.

He watched as she touched the fastenings of her pale green dress with steady fingers. His hands were trembling.

She stood before him, slimly lovely. He welcomed her into his arms.

Her hands had been hot, yet her body was cool. But it wouldn't be for long, he thought, his eager fingers running over the surfaces of her flesh, his lips moving to hers.

As he caressed her, hunger mounted more and more swiftly within him. He drew her closer. He could hear his own labored breathing, could feel the pounding of his heart. And then, suddenly, he realized the girl's breath was measured and even, her heart-beats normal, her body cool and quiet.

He ground his teeth in anger and frustration. What was wrong with him? He dug his fingers into her flesh. Let her cry out, let her scream! Anything was better than this quiet resignation that was beginning to render him impotent.

"Eve," he whispered brokenly, "why can't you—" He bit back the words. This wasn't Eve. This was Mitzi, a girl who had asked for his embrace, whose limbs had pressed so intimately close to his when they had danced.

When he withdrew from her, satiated yet not satisfied, he was murmuring, "Eve." He was with Eve, wasn't he? Not some girl named Mitzi. He was drunk. That was it. He was in the Telegraph Hill apartment and this Hollywood thing was all a dream.

"You hurt me." It wasn't Eve's voice.

He looked at her. Her lower lip was trembling.

"I'm sorry, Mitzi. But, damn it—I wanted to make love to you."

"Well, you did, didn't you? I let you have what you wanted, didn't I?"

He got up and began dressing. "I thought that you—" He paused. "What I mean is, the way you danced with me."

"I just wanted to let you know I was a good sport."

"It wasn't because you really wanted me?" He shook his head, frowning. "Then, why in hell—?"

"Look, in this town, a girl has to be a good sport if she wants to have any fun. Gee, if you turn a man down, he never dates you again."

"So, that's how it is."

"Sure. There are so many girls in this town."

"Competition." He knotted his tie. "I'm curious, Mitzi. Tell me, have your other boy friends ever registered any complaints?"

"What do you mean?"

He didn't reply. Looking down at her, he thought: perhaps for some men this fragile youngness is enough.

Ted was still awake when Mike came in. Grinning, he asked, "Land a job as night watchman somewhere?"

"Don't, Ted. Don't bring up the employment situation right now. I can't take it. These Hollywood boys have me licked."

"Relax, boy. I've got a job for you."

"No!"

"Oh, yes. With Hale, Bradford, Curry, and Stine. A hot-shot advertising agency. In the same class with Wellington and Grant. Anyway, among their accounts are the two biggest television plungers in the country. You'll be handling them and a couple of others as well. Larry Latham, who's been holding the job down, has had to be carted off for a six weeks' rest. You're going to work like hell, boy. But, I think it's just what you need. Work your tail off. Forget everything else for the next month and a half. After that, you can make up your mind as to whether you want to stay on in the game, or—"

"You make it appear as though this job's all lined up. But they haven't even talked to me, haven't even seen me—"

"They've talked to me—and they've heard. I had a long conference with Curry and Stine yesterday and you're in."

"You knew about it this morning! You let me go out and—"

Ted chuckled. "Sure. I thought it would be a good idea for you to get a few Hollywood callouses." He started toward the refrigerator. "Let's have a bottle of beer to celebrate." Opening the beer, Ted winked. "All those smoothies who've been turning you down today will be around with cigars for you tomorrow."

CHAPTER TWELVE

"I GO to these brawls for business reasons only," Ted said as he parked expertly between two long limousines. "And so does just about everybody else, after the first couple of times."

Mike, looking at the brightly lighted mansion, whistled softly.

"Quite a joint, Mike, isn't it? Well, Lura sunk her movie earnings into some oil wells."

"Where's the swimming pool?"

"They're in back. This is a three-pool dump."

As they walked up the stairs, Mike said, "We can pull out of here at a decent hour, I hope. I've a large day ahead of me."

Ted chuckled. "Just give me the high-sign when you're ready to leave, boy."

A young Filipino took their hats at the door and then Ted steered Mike into a baronial drawing room aglow with indirect, rosy lighting. A dozen or so couples were dancing to the soft music of a first-class orchestra while others were clustered about in small groups, talking and gesturing animatedly.

"Rather tame, yet," Ted commented. "But wait until they get tanked up." He glanced about.

Mike guessed that he was looking for their hostess, Lura Leland, a one-time star. In his teens, Mike had seen some of her last, and not too successful, pictures and, even now, could recall her face and figure. Laura Leland, he thought idly, must be well along in her fifties.

"There she is," Ted said, inclining his head toward a woman who was crossing the room with an amazingly handsome young man in tow.

Mike raised his eyebrows. "She doesn't seem to have changed any."

"I'll say she hasn't." Ted stopped. "Oh, you're referring to her appearance. Well, she doesn't look as good in broad daylight, I can tell you that. When I saw her at Santa Anita—"

Lura Leland was coming toward them, her hand uplifted in a graceful little gesture of greeting.

Her eyes wandered over Mike from head to toe. Then, the introductions over, she murmured, "Mike—Mike Carlyle. I like that name." Her voice implied that wasn't all she liked. The young man beside her pouted and said:

"Dahling! You told me you were going to talk to Coe about my test and you know he's going to be here for just a little while."

"I know, Eddie. I'll attend to it right away," she murmured soothingly. And to Mike: "I'll be seeing you."

Ted led Mike to an alcoved bar where several of Lura Leland's guests had congregated. Mike shook hands with a director, a character actor, and a bored-looking girl with eyelashes which seemed to be at least two inches long. Ted had said, "Mike's down from San Francisco, used to be in radio, and—" He didn't have a chance to add that Mike Carlyle was now associated with Hale, Bradford, Curry & Stine. Later, Mike thought it might have made a difference.

But Ted had caught the eye of a short, important-looking man. "Look, Mike, there's someone I want to talk to. Be back in a little while."

And so Mike stood by the bar, now and again trying to include himself in the bizarre conversation of the people around him. They were polite enough, but it was apparent he was regarded as one of the peasantry.

He wandered back to the dance floor and noticed that the music was louder, and so was the laughter. The party was speeding up. A great many more people had arrived. He looked them over. Some of the faces were very familiar. That girl, now, the one standing alone. He moved toward her and said, "Haven't I seen you before—in pictures?"

"Not yet," she said. Then: "What studio are you with?"

"I'm not connected with any of them."

"Oh?" She made no effort to disguise her utter lack of interest in him. Coolly, and most rudely, she turned away.

Shrugging, Mike looked around for Ted. Unable to spot him in the milling mob, he went back to the bar.

He felt much surer of himself after the fourth highball. He grinned at the flaming-haired girl who had just stepped up to the bar. "Dance?"

"Thank you, yes."

They danced silently for a moment and then the girl said, "What studio are you with?"

"I'm in a different racket."

"Oh?" It was the same lilting, meaningful sound he'd heard before. That soft, rising inflection.

Like the lads, Mike thought, these Hollywood lasses have their brush-off technique down pat.

He returned to the bar. There was nothing wrong with the liquor. But he was going to watch himself tonight. Wasn't going to get loaded and have a head in the morning. Just one more drink. One more and he'd get a nice pleasant glow. Then he'd round up Ted and they'd beat it.

"This'll be the last," he was saying to himself at two o'clock.

"Mike, dahling!" It was Lura Leland. "I've been looking for you. Ted had to dash off and he told me to tell you to take the car when you were ready to leave. But you won't be leaving for a while, will you?"

He had slid off the bar stool. She moved closer to him.

A little over-ripe, but—He liked the way she was beginning to cling to him. He lowered his head and, when he brought his mouth close to hers, the tip of her tongue glided over his lips. His blood began warming.

She pulled away, just a little, and tilting her head, looked up at him with half-closed, inviting eyes.

"Lord, you're a lovely wench." Why, he thought, she couldn't be a day more than thirty-five. Maybe she had been in pictures a long time, but she'd been just a kid when she started.

"Mike Carlyle—" Her voice caressed him. He saw the rise and fall of her breasts as she began breathing faster. Once again, her hips pressed against him.

"I'd like to have you alone with me, baby," he said huskily.

"Let's go upstairs," she whispered.

They started from the alcove. An amused voice reached his ears: "He's the third one tonight."

For an instant, Mike had the impression that the remark had to do with him. Then, he dismissed the thought. It didn't make sense, did it? ... *the third one tonight—*

When Mike wakened, dawn was dimly lighting the room. He groaned as the old, familiar stabbing pain went through his head. So, he'd done it again. Got himself stinking drunk.

He began realizing, then, that it hadn't been the morning light which wakened him. Soft hands.

Lura Leland's hands. He began remembering. They'd come upstairs and—he smiled.

Still smiling, he turned.

"Mike," she murmured.

The smile froze on his lips. He looked at her, appalled. Gray lips flecked with remains of lipstick, caked make-up which accentuated the deep lines about her mouth and the network of wrinkles about her bloodshot eyes. What a hag this was.

She was hovering over him, her long, sagging breasts dangling obscenely.

"I've got to leave," he muttered. "I've a business appointment."

"It's early—it's only about six."

"I tell you I've got to get out of here." He flung back the covers and leaped from the bed.

She clawed at him frantically as he tried to pick up his clothing which lay strewn about on the white rug. "Mike!"

He pushed her aside. Somehow, some way, he managed to get into his trousers, slip into his shoes. With his shirt unbuttoned and with his coat over one arm, he ran from her room, down the wide circular stairway and, finally, out into the clean, cool morning air.

He saw Ted's car in the driveway. He remembered how Ted had gone off with the important-looking guy. Getting into the car, Mike wondered why he couldn't be like Ted. Why couldn't he keep his mind on business? Why didn't he know when to stop drinking?

"Damn it, I've got to straighten out. If I don't, I'll sure as hell wind up in Skid Row."

Sally Kaye stared at the telephone. *Tonight. You'll call me tonight, won't you, Mike? You were still angry yesterday, that's why you didn't phone. And you didn't call me at the station today because you were afraid Hazel—or somebody—might listen in.*

The hands of the clock on the mantle were creeping closer and closer together. Twenty-one minutes to eight.

Maybe—maybe Mike wasn't going to call. Maybe he believed she had the strength of character to live up to her resolution.

Oh, Mike, I was a fool! I should have been satisfied with what you were willing to give me. I shouldn't have let my pride stand in the way. It won't ever happen again, Mike. Never! I've no pride left. I've nothing left except love for you.

With a little sobbing cry, she picked up the telephone, dialed Mike's number.

He isn't home. He's gone somewhere with someone else.

And then, a voice, "That number has been disconnected."

"No, it can't be! There must be some mistake!"

"No, madame."

"Operator—wait a minute. Can you get me the apartment manager's telephone number?"

"If you'll give me the address, I will see."

Moments later, Sally put down the phone, the clipped sentences still echoing in her ears, "Mr. Carlyle sub-let his apartment. He's left town. He didn't say where he was going."

He's gone to Hollywood—to Eve.

It was, Sally thought, a kind of living death, this going on, day after day, with the knowledge that Mike was lost to her. *I've got to snap out of it. When my vacation starts next month, I'll go where I'll see new faces and I'll leave all these memories behind me. I'll go to Tahoe. No, it's too late in the season. A dude ranch, maybe…*

She put down her highball and said, "'Bye, Izzy."

"Not leaving so soon, are you?" That was Hank Walton. "You can't do that to me. Here I am, just coming in and you start going out."

"I've things to do at home. I'm getting ready for my vacation."

Walton leered. "Spending your two weeks in Hollywood, eh?"

She looked at him, frowning. "Just what do you mean by that crack?"

Unabashed, he said "Well, word's got around that Mike's down there and since Eve's lit out for Reno—"

"Eve's gone to Reno?" Her voice trembled.

"As if you didn't know! There was an item about it in *The Spotlight* and—" He broke off, grinning at the expression on her face. "Say, I guess you haven't seen it at that." He reached into his overcoat pocket. "Have a look, sweetheart."

Sally took the paper and read: RADIO WARBLER RENO-BOUND—

Hank chortled. "I said, all along, it wouldn't last. Eve's too good for that chippy chaser. Like I was telling Harry today—" The words kept on cascading, but Sally didn't hear anything he said.

It's all over between them now! It's over and done with. And maybe if I go to Hollywood—maybe Mike and I—

CHAPTER THIRTEEN

OR THE past ten days, Mike had been driving himself furiously. The long hours, the constant challenges. They'd been good for him, he reflected. Ted had been right. This is what he needed.

Ted, bless him, was always right about everything.

By the time Eve returned from Reno, he'd be a new man. She'd be able to see that. And the rift between them would be cleared up. She was his wife. Six weeks and a legal document from Nevada wouldn't alter that fact. He'd said as much to Ted.

And Ted had smiled peculiarly. "I never thought I'd ever see you hooked as completely as this. That gal must have everything."

Ted doesn't know. And, even if I could talk about it to him, I couldn't explain it. I can't understand it myself. Unless, maybe, it's the Pygmalion instinct—the desire to mold a woman, to dedicate your talents to the enhancing of her, to bring her to utter perfection.

"Have a beer, Mike?"

"Not even a small one. I've reformed, feller. And, look at the time! Eleven-thirty. I've got a conference scheduled early tomorrow morning."

There were conferences nearly every morning for Mike, too. And battles nearly every day with agents of film celebrities and near-celebrities. And unending skirmishes with sponsors.

When a sponsor decided that a certain singer should handle a vocal chore and Mike felt that someone else had wider appeal, it meant a long verbal combat which he didn't always win.

On one occasion, Stine said, "I don't think you're going to get very far with old man King. He wants longer commercials and he isn't easily budged."

"I'm going to try," Mike said, grinning.

An hour later, he was talking to the soup manufacturer who paid a fabulous price for *Hollywood Follies,* a coast-to-coast TV show. "I realize how it is, Mr. King. You never get tired of hearing how good your products are—because you know they are good and you feel that nobody can say too much for them. But, you aren't the audience sitting out in front of the television screen. You aren't the fellow who pays out his eighteen cents for your product. So, you've got to make an effort to imagine—"

"I know. I know, Carlyle. But look here. Commercials can be really interesting. For instance, couldn't you have a girl-can and a boy-can. They could have a little conversation and then do a dance or something. Anyhow, you get the idea, don't you? I want those commercials longer! It's always been our advertising policy to pound our trade name into the minds of the potential buyers. It's got us sales in the past."

"Your billboard and newspaper advertising has been highly successful. But, with radio and television, you're in a different media. Audiences accept the fact that they have to listen to some advertising to get some entertainment, but that doesn't make them like it. How would you like it, if you went to see some fine performance and, in the middle of a scene, a spieler stepped out to the front of the stage to bark about canned beans?"

When Mike finally arose to take his departure, King said, "Tell Stine that the commercials will run their usual length."

That meant a full seven minutes out of a half-hour program would be devoted to extolling the soup that was *Fit for a King.* But, Mike had won something; he'd talked King out of lengthening the plugs.

"Nice work," Stine said later. "King has been yessed so much, he's practically impossible to reason with any more. Damned glad you were able to handle him, Mike. *Hollywood Follies* is too good a show to ruin with eulogies about canned soups."

"What a day!" Mike said, striding into Ted's living room. "Yakked half the morning with old man King. Got tied up this afternoon with that flesh peddler, Crawford. Had to have dinner with the guy. He's a smart little ten-percenter, isn't he?"

"I've a hunch he didn't outsmart you, boy." Ted grinned. "I've been hearing things about you. Ball of fire, aren't you?"

"Work kind of agrees with me. I'm beginning to be afraid I'll wind up being an old man with no interest in life except making money and worrying about the condition of my bowels."

"We can't let that happen. You come along with me tonight. There's a brawl at Lamont's."

"Not for me. I'm bushed." Mike flung himself into an easy chair. "I'm staying home with a good book." He reached for a volume on the table alongside. "I'm going to read for an hour and then I'm hitting the sack."

Hardly more than twenty minutes after Ted had left, the telephone jangled. Mike retrieved it from under a pile of magazines.

"Hello" he answered.

A soft voice said, "Hello, Ted, I'm looking for Mike. Would you know where the lug is?"

"Sally?"

"Oh, Mike! I flew in just a while ago and—"

"Where are you staying? Oh, the Sunset. Well, I'll be seeing you as soon as I can get over there."

It was strange, he thought, putting down the phone. A few minutes ago, he'd been thinking about calling it a night and getting some sleep. But now—why, he'd never felt so wide-awake in his life.

Gee, it would be good to see Sally again!

She was waiting for him in the lobby. She rose when she saw him and came toward him.

He caught his breath. She seemed paler and a little thinner than he had remembered, but he had never seen her looking any lovelier.

"Sally—" He kissed her instinctively, then hastily drew back. *Keep your head, Mike. Remember Eve. Those six weeks are up and, any day now, Ted will be saying, "Eve was down at Continental today."*

He took Sally's arm. "We're going places tonight. This calls for a celebration."

There were highballs at the Sunset bar, Mexican lobster at the Brown Derby, Singapore slings at the Tahitian, and dancing at the Ambassador.

"You've changed, Mike," Sally said softly as they were guided to a table in the Rhythm Club. "It's not only the way you've been drinking—slowly and carefully—"

"I have changed, Sally. Trying to, anyway." Yet, even as he said it, he wondered. Deliberately, he had refrained from holding her close, but even the slightest contact with her body disturbed him. He manufactured a grin and said. "I'm a businessman, now. Strictly business."

"There's something else. Or—is it someone else?" Her gaze was searching.

He glanced away. He couldn't say, "I'm going back to Eve." Yet, if he didn't tell her now, he might not be able to say it later. Already, his pulses were beginning to race, his yearning for her was increasing every second. She'd flown south to be with him, but only because she thought that Eve was out of his life. He knew how it was with her. She'd made it plain that time in San Francisco.

"Sally, this is a dismal joint."

"Why, Mike, it seems to be quite a spot. Haven't you noticed all the celebrities?"

A waiter was hovering over them. "Two scotch highballs," Mike said. He looked back at Sally. "As soon as we finish them let's pull out of here. H'm?"

Her hand touched his and she nodded.

If she knew I was going back to Eve, she wouldn't take me to her room. But I've got to have her just one more time.

He watched her lift her drink and then, out of the corner of his eye, he saw the couple standing in the entrance way. A man of distinction escorting an exquisite golden girl.

"Why, Mike, what's the matter?" Sally turned, following the direction of his stare. Eve Tremaine waved a greeting and, with Harvey Terris at her heels, came toward the table.

Automatically, Mike got to his feet. "Hello, Eve. Hello, Terris. Why, yes, Eve. We'd be happy to have you join us." The words were coming out of him as though he'd turned on a switch.

Eve said, "I've worn Harvey out. You know me, Mike, when it comes to dancing. You won't mind, will you, Sally, if I make Mike dance with me?"

Sally murmured, "I wouldn't mind—why should I?"

Mike took Eve in his arms. What a little girl she was. So eager to sing and dance. He looked down at the golden head.

"I just got back Mike. I intended to call you the first thing tomorrow morning. I wanted to—to explain things."

"You were really going to call me? Oh, my darling!"

"I wanted to have a long talk with you, Mike. I'm staying at the Stanford and if you'd come over tomorrow about five-thirty… Please say that you will, Mike."

"Of course, I will." Tenderly, his lips touched her soft, fragrant hair.

A few moments after they had returned to their table, Harvey Terris gave Eve a significant glance. "Look who's here."

Mike saw the hulking figure bearing down on them. He recognized the advertising agency executive with whom Eve had stayed out until dawn.

Carrol Black's face was flushed with either rage or alcohol. "You little bitch—" Thick fingers went about Eve's wrist. She was jerked to her feet.

Mike had pushed back his chair, but Terris was nearer. He sought to pull Carrol Black aside, but was shoved back violently. As Terris stumbled, Mike stepped in and grasped Black's shoulder.

"Keep out of my way," the advertising agency executive snarled. His fist flashed out toward Mike's chin.

Mike dodged the blow and let Black have it right between the third and fourth vest buttons. The big man teetered back on his heels. Mike gripped his collar and shoved him into a flying wedge of waiters who were hurrying to quell the disturbance.

"Thank you, Mike," Eve whispered. "You were simply wonderful."

Harvey Terris said, "Look, Eve, you told me you wanted to be home by midnight and it's a quarter of, now."

"Quarter of!" she echoed. "You're simply going to have to break the speed limit getting me home, Harvey. I simply must have my eight hours' sleep if I'm going to be in good voice tomorrow."

Mike watched Eve and Terris go.

Sally said softly, "It's still Eve, isn't it?" She had moved closer to him and he was very conscious of the faint but exciting fragrance of her, Maybe, if he pretended he had not heard her—

No. He had to be honest with her, this time.

"I want you terribly, Sally, but I'm still in love with Eve. And I can't have it both ways."

"Yes, you can. I haven't any pride left, Mike."

"Sally, do you know what you're saying?"

She reached for her handbag. "Let's leave, Mike."

Eve knew perfectly well that she didn't mean anything in particular to Terris, that she was, so to speak, just a part of his harem. Not even that, if you got right down to it. She was no more than an adventure to him, a transient excitement to him; he would tire of her quickly, no doubt, and return to his regular concubines, like that Rita Yolanda who had appeared as a star in two spectaculars—or Marietta Ming, the aging but still superbly attractive Oriental actress who some years before had taken Hollywood by storm. It was well known in sophisticated Beverly Hills circles that these were his enduring choices, and that in his way Terris was more or less faithful to them, even if he did engage in escapades with kids like Eve once in a while.

If I'm going to use him, I'll have to make it fast, thought Eve. *Before he gets bored with me.* Terris had just left. It was four in the morning. But Eve did not go to sleep. She sat in a soft chair, bit her lip, and cogitated deeply.

Marietta Ming—that was it! Marietta was known to be a close friend not only of Terris, but of Womack, the all-powerful producer whose name was currently magic. And another thing was whispered about Marietta. She was supposed to be odd in some of her ways.

Having planned her course of action, Eve contentedly sought her bed. In a few moments she was sleeping peacefully and deeply, like an innocent child.

At noon the next day, upon rising, she immediately telephoned Terris, made a date to meet him for lunch at two. She joined him at the *Brown Derby,* looking fresh as a daisy and full of glowing health. As she consumed a poached egg, she managed to wheedle him into promising to introduce her to the glamorous Marietta Ming. "I was an admirer of hers even while I was still in high school," Eve told him breathlessly. "I'm dying to meet her. You know her so well, they say, Harvey. You could arrange it."

Terris looked at her, noted the stars in her eyes, phony or otherwise, and nodded. Why not? What would it cost him?

And so it happened that Eve one sunny afternoon visited Marietta's Beverly Hills estate, by invitation.

Over cups of fragrant tea in an elegant drawing room, blue-eyed Eve stared at her sloe-eyed hostess. Marietta had chosen to greet her visitor in a pair of form-hugging silken slacks, topped by a loose embroidered blouse that looked as if it were made in Hong Kong, which indeed it was. Eve noted that Marietta was much taller and fuller in the figure than most Chinese girls. But the face of the actress was as delicate and as finely formed as a lotus bloom. The faint perfume of some unknown flower seemed to rise from her ivory skin. Her hair, sleek and black, was coiled high on her head and held in place by an amber comb. Pendant drops of ivory hung from her ear lobes. Her cherry lips glistened. She was supposed to be well over forty. She looked not a day older than seventeen.

They chatted about acting and actors, about directors and producers, about singers and dancers. Eve, quite cleverly, led the conversation to Marietta's early days in Hollywood, thus giving the woman plenty of chance to talk, for she loved to reminisce. After a while, Marietta said:

"You really are a darling, to listen so patiently to my tales. And clever, too."

Eve set down her tea cup. She rose from her chair, proceeded to strut about the luxurious room, bending over here to examine a jade vase, reaching up there to look at a volume in a towering bookcase. Actually, she was carefully displaying her points, like a peacock. Calmly, she said, "Clever?"

"Yes, my dear," Marietta answered in her musical but brittle contralto. "You seek to ingratiate yourself by piquing me into talk, then acting the part of the good listener. You parade yourself before me, as if to intrigue me with your form. Tell me, my pretty Eve, what are you after?"

For a moment, and for the first time, Eve was taken aback. "I—I am not after anything, Miss Ming. Why, I—I just wanted to meet you."

"So Harvey told me," Marietta said. Unhurriedly, she looked Eve up and down, inspecting the long, silky legs, the vibrant body clad in a pink cotton frock, the lovely face with its perpetual air of innocence, the honey-blonde tresses arranged in crisp curls.

Marietta's eyes were enigmatic. "Do not be embarrassed, child. Who is it among us that does not have some axe to grind?" She too rose from her chair. "It is lovely outside, so bright and yet balmy. Shall we try the pool?"

"Oh, I'd love to. But I have no suit," Eve responded eagerly.

"Unnecessary. In my pool, we cannot be observed."

Eve hesitated. That would be moving too fast. She still put some value on her pose of innocent youth, innocent youth sullied by men such as Terris, perhaps, but still knowing nothing of romance in its more exotic forms. "Oh—I'm afraid not. I wouldn't want to swim without a suit, Miss Ming." Eve bit down on her tongue and so managed a bit of a blush. It made her look adorable.

"Call me Marietta," said the hostess. "All right, then. Come upstairs and we'll find you suitable attire. Anything," she finished wryly, "for a friend of Harvey's."

They climbed a luxurious flight of stairs. In a loft-ceilinged, airy bedroom, filled with trinkets of the East and an enormous, custom-built bed, Marietta led the way to a closet. When she opened the sliding doors, Eve saw on hangers a collection of at least two dozen bathing suits.

"What would you like? Bikini? A dressmaker style?"

"You're so much taller than I," said Eve, suppressing a gasp at the sight of the finery. "Would they fit me?"

"There are a number of sizes there," Marietta said. Her voice had lost its brittle timbre. It sounded warm and husky.

Still Eve hesitated.

Marietta smiled. "Perhaps you would prefer to try them on in privacy. Choose the one you wish, then join me at the pool. Turn left at the foot of the stairs and walk through to the patio. You can't miss it." So saying, she seemed to glide out of the room.

A few minutes later, attired in a white Bikini, Eve joined her hostess at poolside. Marietta wore a black singlet, of dull, translucent silk, and a perfect foil for the ivory of her skin. With a laugh, Marietta launched herself from the diving board into the clear water. Eve plunged in. Soon the two were cavorting and giggling and splashing like children, stopping every now and then to rest and warm themselves in the sun. In the water, Eve was boisterously playful, catching at Marietta from behind as the Chinese girl glided silkily through the wavelets, and trying to spill or duck her. Or Eve would approach under water, seized Marietta's wet legs, drag her down, and while Marietta sputtered and gasped, the coltish Eve would twist away, laughing. Marietta soon got into the spirit of the thing, trying tricks of her own. And so did they gambol and lark and play, until Marietta, having taken aboard a gulletful of water when Eve had suddenly up-ended her, climbed exhausted out of the pool. "Oh, you brat. You naughty child, you. Is that a way to treat your elders?"

Eve, a nymph in a white Bikini, climbed up the ladder and stood before Marietta. "I haven't had so much fun in years," said Eve.

"Nor have I. But what a mischievous little thing you are!"

"I guess I just ought to be spanked," Eve answered with a grin.

"Yes. And I'm the one to do it."

"You've got to catch me first!" And Eve was off, racing to the other side of the pool. Marietta followed, lithe and lovely, ducking this way and that, trying to trap Eve. After a few moments, Eve allowed herself to be cornered. Marietta, screaming and giggling, delivered a resounding thwack to the hips. In a moment the two were struggling and heaving, Marietta trying to throw Eve to the grassy ground. This attempt was successful. Eve went down, prone, Marietta falling across her. Marietta slapped with strange enthusiasm. Her sloe eyes now were glittering. Her breath was coming harshly. Suddenly her legs locked around Eve's palpitating body.

"Oh, you naughty darling. You little darling!" said Marietta.

"Just a minute!" Eve wriggled, heaved, threw off the Chinese woman.

"Well, don't act so indignant," said Marietta. "All afternoon, you've been deliberately teasing and tempting me. I don't know what your game is—but you've won it. So put aside that coyness, and tell me what the stakes are."

Eve jumped to her feet.

"All right. I want an introduction to Basil Womack. I want you to tell him that from afar, I've acquired a terrific crush on him. I—I want you to say that I would gladly be his slave."

"You'll have to be mine first," said Marietta.

Eve laughed, and dropped to the turf. She rolled over on her back and looked up at the other, her blue eyes wonderfully innocent, and her lips half parted in wicked invitation.

Marietta, in her silken suit, drew a passionate, sighing breath. Then her cherry mouth descended, and found its goal.

As Eve felt seeking her own mouth the soft lips and darting tongue of the other, memory jogged. Eve was grateful now that once the pretty Mexican girl, Conchita, not to mention Agatha, had unfolded certain mysteries. Men were so coarse and loutish. But this—this was the path to true ecstasy.

Eve returned Marietta's kiss, urgently, thirstily.

"Naughty girl," cooed Marietta. Her hands fondled. Fire seemed to spread through Eve's veins.

The next morning, in her shower, Sally let the cold needle-pointed spray play over her body and felt her nipples harden just as they had under the warmth of Mike's hands.

"Mike," she breathed, remembering his last embrace at dawn. How reluctant he had been to leave. *I'm going to call the office and cancel all morning appointments.* That's what he had said.

"No, darling." It hadn't been easy, but she had forced herself to go on: "You must leave now, my dearest. Get back to Ted's and shave and make like a brilliant young executive. I'll be waiting for you tonight."

Toweling herself dry, she walked over to the bed and sank down. It was wonderful, she thought, this feeling of complete relaxation. She leaned back, stretching luxuriously.

The telephone jangled. Her eyes went to the traveling clock on her bureau. Twenty past nine. It couldn't be Mike. He had a nine o'clock conference. But—who else could it be? Nobody knew she was in Hollywood.

She lifted the receiver gingerly.

"Hello?"

"Hi, this is Ted."

"Oh."

"Is that all you can say to an old pal?"

"Well, this is something of a surprise. I didn't know you knew I was in town.

"Mike woke me up before he left this morning. Told me he saw you last night and that you're going to be around for a while."

"For a couple of weeks."

"Would you be interested in staying considerably longer? Look, Sally, I don't know if Mike mentioned it, but I'm handling public relations for Continental."

"Why, that's grand, Ted!"

"Yeah, but what isn't so grand is that I've had no luck getting a really competent gal Friday. Now, you know every angle of this publicity business, and if the climate agrees with you—"

"It sounds interesting, but—look, let me think."

"I know. This is so sudden, huh? Well, I'll give you plenty of time. You can tell me 'yes' at one o'clock. I'll call for you and we'll have lunch together."

She sat next to Ted in the zebra-skin upholstered banquette. He glanced at his watch. "One-thirty, and you still haven't answered me."

"You're making that opening for me at Continental, aren't you?"

"I—" He broke off and darted her a probing glance. "Oh, all right. What if I am?"

"Quit horsing around, Ted. Give it to me straight."

He didn't answer immediately. He toyed with his fork. Then putting it down, he said slowly. "It's like this. I've found out that Eve's been back in town for a couple of days. She's been checking up on Mike. That little trollop might be thinking about using Mike again. She's probably learned that he's coming along fast, that he's getting to know a lot of the right people and is putting himself over with some very important gents. She might even be planning to re-marry him. If she does, she'll stop his clock for good. He'll blow his top, Sally, if he ever finds out. You know how Mike is."

"I know."

"There's a wide streak of idealism in Mike's make-up. That accounts for ninety-nine per cent of his feeling for Eve. To him, she symbolizes feminine purity. Know what I mean? Anyway, when an idealist gets a swift kick in the pants, he's apt to go off his rocker. Now, Mike isn't a violent sort of guy but plenty of other guys no more violent than he, have been driven to murder."

Sally nodded. "I can see what you mean. If Eve ever played around—"

"Hell! She certainly has been playing around. And, she's a smart little tart. She's learning fast. She won't make any more mistakes like she did when she hooked Black."

Sally stared down at her half-finished salad.

Ted said with a thin smile, "You probably haven't been around here long enough to've heard the whole story. Well, Carrol Black talked his wife into getting a Mexican divorce. He couldn't take off time for a six weeks' Reno trip. But, there was one thing both Eve and Carrol overlooked. Mrs. Black is Sam Wellington's daughter. And so, now, Carrol is no longer with Wellington and

Grant, and, from the looks of things, he won't connect anywhere else. Sam Wellington's going to see to it that the guy is kaput in this burg."

"Eve still has Harvey Terris."

"Yeah, she's one of his harem. There's a mutual exchange of favors, but he has other obligations in other directions. And Eve wants to shove ahead fast. She's been fooling around with Basil Womack. Know who he is, don't you?"

"He's top producer and director at New World Films, isn't he?"

"Yep. And so, Eve's getting a screen test out at New World today. Basil doesn't arrange those for free."

They were thoughfully silent for a moment, then Ted went on, "Mike's been dreaming about patching up things with Eve and, if it suits her purposes, she'll marry him again. But the little idyll won't last long. Mike's bound to find out something, and then, boom! The front pages will headline another shooting—or suicide."

With trembling fingers, Sally lifted a glass of water to her lips. She sipped and, over the rim, looked into Ted's anxious eyes. "Would my staying change anything?"

"There's a good chance that it might. He cares for you, Sally. It's the real thing, even if he doesn't know it, yet."

"Do you really believe that, Ted?"

"I know it. I've been close to that guy for years. It's not what he's said, but what he has left unsaid, that makes me absolutely sure. Get an apartment, quick, Sally. Set up a little domestic scene and make him move in with you. Intellectually, he's been fighting against being a husband. But, at heart, that's what he wants to be. Maybe, he hates the bourgeois sound of the word *home,* but he longs for one, just the same. He keeps remembering that brief time with Eve."

"I remember, too." She had thought it was Eve that was good for him, "I think I can understand things better, now."

"Then you'll remain in Hollywood?"

"I was planning on staying anyway, Ted. I didn't say yes because I wanted to find out a few things. I learned even more than I expected." She pressed his hand gratefully. "I think you're right about Mike. Maybe, if we had really lived together in San Francisco instead of just going to bed together—Know where I can find an apartment, Ted? I don't want to lose any time. He ran into Eve last night."

Ted swore under his breath.

"But she went off with Terris. She didn't have a chance to say very much to Mike. And, if she's having a screen test today—"

Ted pulled at his lower lip. "It might be a week before she makes a pitch. Come on, Sally. We're going house-hunting."

CHAPTER FOURTEEN

IT WAS exactly five-thirty.

"Right on time!" Eve exclaimed, holding out her hands to him.

"Eve," Mike murmured. How beautiful she was, he thought; how young and exquisitely virginal.

She led him to the divan and sat close to him. "It's wonderful, Mike, seeing you again." There was a pathetic trembling to her lips, a candent glowing in her eyes.

He said, none too steadily: "Eve, you still care for me, don't you?"

"Of course, Mike. I've never stopped loving you for a moment."

He looked at her incredulously. "And yet, you left me."

"Only because that's what you wanted me to do."

"I wanted ... Whatever do you mean, Eve?"

"Why—why the way you talked to me that morning in San Francisco, I thought you wanted your freedom, and so—"

He put his hands on her shoulders. "My poor little girl! Didn't you realize I was out of my mind with jealousy. I'd seen you with Black and—"

"You were jealous?" Her eyes widened. "Oh, no. You couldn't have been. Why, Carrol's old enough to be my father. He's nearly fifty."

"You'd stayed out with him until dawn."

"But, that didn't mean anything. I tried to explain how it was, how we'd all been sitting around talking, paying no attention to the time."

"I could understand that, Eve. But when I saw you kiss him—"

She nodded and lowered her eyelashes. "I shouldn't have. I know that, now." She sighed deeply. "It was a terrible mistake in more ways than one. I just meant to be friendly, and I thought he would understand it that way. But ever since then, well, I've had a terrible time avoiding him. You saw how he was last night."

Mike lifted her hand to his lips. "You've so much to learn, little Eve."

She nestled closer, putting her golden head on his shoulder. He smiled. *I'm going to be able to win her back. But I'll not affront her with impatience. I'll woo her carefully.*

She said, "You're right, Mike. I'm simply lost here in Hollywood. You know how much a career means to me, but I can't seem to get what I want. For instance, I happened to hear about a TV show where there's a wonderful opening for a girl singer, but I wouldn't even know how to go about trying for it. If you could give me some advice, Mike—"

"What show is it?"

"*Hollywood Follies—that* soup show."

His laughter rang out. "Well, I'll be—of course! There haven't been any final decisions yet and—" *There was more than an even chance he could put it over. King liked him. And, if he worked an angle or two—*

"Now, look, Eve. I can't promise anything." He paused.

The puzzled expression on her face was quite dramatic.

"I forgot to tell you," he said portentously. "I'm with Hale, Bradford, Curry and Stine, you know."

"Yes?" She was still obviously puzzled.

What a babe in the woods she was. He lifted her chin in his cupped palm and smiling into her lovely face said, "I'm with the agency that's handling the King account."

"Oh." It was as though she could hardly believe it.

His lips touched her cheek reverently. "I'll see what I can work out." Because she wanted it so much—a really big opportunity—he would give it to her. He was a suitor, now; he would bestow the gifts she longed for. Yet, need there be a long courtship? Maybe, if he asked her right now, she would respond as he wanted her to.

The telephone rang. With a murmured "It just might be important," Eve drew away and stood up.

She crossed the room and, lifting the receiver, held it close to her ear. "Yes?"

Mike watched her, wondering if it were a man who was talking to her. He heard her speak again. "Oh, no. I haven't forgotten."

Whoever it was calling went on a bit longer. Then Eve said, "Just the same, I'm awfully glad you called. Yes. Goodbye, for now." There'd been a purring quality to her voice but when she turned back to Mike she was laughing like a naughty child.

"I told a fib, Mike. Honestly, I'd forgotten all about it. You see, that was my dramatic coach on the phone. He was afraid I'd forgotten I had an appointment for a lesson tonight. And I had forgotten, all right. I'm simply going to have to dash."

"Can I drive you?"

"Oh, no, Mike. I'll have to change and, darling, you'll have to run along. But we'll see each other tomorrow night, won't we?"

It was nearly seven-thirty when Mike walked in. Ted said, "Where've you been, boy? Sally just called. You have a date with her tonight."

"I'm going to have to break it. Want to talk to King. Haven't been able to contact him yet."

"Now, look, sticking to business is highly commendable, but—"

"This thing won't wait, Ted. I'll have to work fast. I intend to get Eve that open spot in the *Follies*."

Ted got up from the chair where he had been sitting. "So that's where you've been. With Eve."

"Yes. We had a long talk. That poor little kid. You know, she took off for Reno only because she thought I wanted to be free."

Narrowing his eyes, Ted said, "Figuring on going back to her, huh?"

"If she'll have me." Mike smiled. "And, I think she will. Matter of fact, I'm pretty sure. The way—" He broke off. "Why are you giving me that funny look. Don't you approve of marriage?"

"I think it's a damned fine institution for some people, especially guys like you. It isn't marriage I disapprove of."

"Am I to infer that you disapprove of Eve? If so, you can shut your big mouth. I'm not interested in anything you have to say about her."

"See here, Mike, if I saw a truck bearing down on you, I'd jerk you out of its way. I'd even risk getting myself hurt. And you can bop me on the jaw if you like, but I'm going to tell you a few things."

"You can stop right there, Ted."

"I could, but I won't. I'm not going to stand by and watch you mess up your life. Listen to me, Mike. In the first place, Eve didn't get a divorce because she thought you were the one who wanted it. She went off to Reno strictly because of Carrol Black."

Mike smiled scornfully: "That shows how much you know about it. Black doesn't mean a thing to her. I saw the guy last night. If she wanted him, he'd come crawling."

"She doesn't want him any more. Not since father-in-law Wellington worked him out with his meat-axe."

"That just some damned Hollywood gossip. You don't know it for a fact."

"I know. I'm in a position to know. I handle Continental's publicity, don't I? And you're as well aware as I am that a publicity man's job isn't only drum-beating. It's hushing things up, too. Tremaine's giving us a headache. Not because of Black, but because of Terris. Terris was flying up to Reno on alternate week-ends."

"Why, you dirty—"

"I'm not the dirty party. Listen to me, Mike. Terris and Black are only part of it. Womack gave her a screen test today. And anybody in the know will be able to tell you where she'll be tonight."

"The foul-mouthed bastards! It so happens I know what she's doing tonight. I was there when her dramatic coach phoned and reminded her of her appointment."

"Dramatic coach! That's good! Womack will be coaching her, all right, in his bedroom."

Mike's fist caught Ted squarely on the jaw. Ted went down, crashing into an end table. He pulled himself up to a sitting position and, gingerly rubbing his chin, muttered, "Lucky I rolled with the punch."

"Shut up!" Mike's eyes were blazing. "I'm clearing out of here—tonight. I'll come back for my things tomorrow; when you're not here."

He stormed out, slamming the door behind him.

In a little bar on Vine Street, he ordered a double scotch. Another. Then another. These damned scandalmongers, he kept thinking. Well, he hadn't been in Hollywood very long but anyway it had been long enough to find out that blasting reputations was a favorite sport. Prurient-minded old women of both sexes would have a field day with someone like Eve whose inherent innocence was something they couldn't comprehend. Because Eve, in her naivete, would kiss a man in public, nasty minds would immediately conjure up the things she might do in private.

And she was so defenseless against these vicious attacks. She was a young and beautiful girl living alone, going out with men.

She couldn't go on living alone. He put down his drink and his glance went to the telephone booth in the far corner. Eve still cared for him. He could tell it from the way she had behaved. He really wouldn't have to woo her. If he said, "Eve, let's get married again—"

He glanced at his wristwatch. Eight forty-five. He wondered how long she'd be with her dramatic coach. There was a good possibility she was through now.

Beckoning the bartender, he said, "One more."

"Takin' 'em kind of fast, fella."

"I'm celebrating. I'm getting married."

"Tonight? Gonna fly to Las Vegas?"

Fly to Las Vegas! That was an idea.

He drained his glass, went to the booth and closed the door behind him. Dropping a coin in the slot, he dialed Eve's number. He listened to the ringing signal. It went on and on. With a sigh, he replaced the receiver. Well, it was still early.

Returning to the bar, he said, "Another one, Mac—"

The bartender grinned. "Fella, you sure can hold it. You not only talk straight, but you walk straight. You walked over to that phone booth like you hadn't even had one drink."

Ted had called Sally at five minutes of eight. "Mike just pulled out of here. He'd seen Eve, and I lost my head, Sally. Couldn't keep my mouth shut any longer. I gave him the works. Even told him she was shacking up with Womack tonight."

"And?" Her voice was tremulous.

"And he socked me on the jaw. I've hashed things up, I'm afraid. Damn it, I'm sorry."

"Poor Ted."

"Yeah. And poor Mike. Well, I thought I'd better tell you that he wouldn't be heading your way tonight. Knowing Mike, I figure he'll make for the nearest bar and try to get in touch with Eve. Then, when he can't reach her, he'll get himself good and crocked."

CHAPTER FIFTEEN

A T EIGHT o'clock, Basil Womack had called for Eve, had led her to his custom-built sedan. He didn't ask where she'd prefer to dine. He took her to a far less glamorous and less crowded spot than she would have chosen. One where they were not likely to meet anyone they knew.

"I want you all to myself this evening, Eve," he explained, appraising her from under hooded eyelids.

She regarded him with an angelic smile, reflecting: *no wonder he's a success. There's such a ruthless competence about him. Even his features, the beaked nose and the hard thin line that is his mouth, proclaim it.*

As they walked toward their table and she caught the expressions of the faces of the people they passed, her eyes glinted with amusement. She knew what they were thinking, Beauty and the Beast. But what a competent little old beast he was!

She wondered if her screen test had come off well. She'd been just a trifle nervous, but she felt she had not done at all badly. Womack had been marvelously helpful. And he would continue to be helpful if she played her cards right, if she played the right game with this notorious old lecher.

No wide-eyed fright for Womack. He wanted something much more piquant.

As she chatted lightly with him, she thought: *It's fortunate I've had a course of instruction from Harvey Terris.* Physically, the two men were utterly unlike but she sensed their kinship; they both craved the exotic; both men wanted something different.

Consulting her only with an occasional glance, Womack ordered dinner. Then, as they ate, and drank champagne, he spoke of her future. "You have talent and you have beauty."

"And so have many other girls." *And, maybe I might be able to get to the top all by myself. But—I'm not taking any chances.*

When he helped her into his car, he didn't mention their destination. But she knew they were bound for his house in Beverly Hills. A show-place, that's what she'd heard people say about it.

Yet, that didn't prepare her for its magnificence. For a moment or two, she was thoroughly overwhelmed. Then, she thought: *Some day, I'll have a house like this, and the sight-seeing buses will pass by and the driver will point and shout my name.*

"Like it, Eve?"

She nodded, her eyes lingering on the lavish décor, her glance going to the expensive paintings. She was very conscious of the deep-piled rug as she walked along at Womack's side.

The butler who had opened the door vanished discreetly. Womack's arm went about her as he led her up the wide stairway. Reaching the top of the stairs, he turned to the right. Eve glimpsed two superbly appointed bedrooms. Womack went on to the end of the hall, pushed open a closed door.

She stepped into a glowing room. Its walls were paneled with mirrors. The ceiling was mirrored. The floor was strewn with thick rugs. There were no windows.

Downstairs in the reception hall, a clock chimed the hour. It was just ten.

Sally stared dully at her clock. Ten-thirty. And no word from Mike.

Ted had phoned less than twenty minutes ago, "I've checked, Sally. Eve isn't home, thank God! Otherwise, he'd be over there on his bended knees. The way he stomped out of here like a knight in shining armor, so damned sure of his lady's purity, he just might have been able to talk her into an elopement."

"He'll try tomorrow."

"Sure, he will, but he'll have one of those Grade A hangovers. He isn't apt to be so persuasive and, in my opinion, the lady isn't quite ready to hook up with him again. I think she wants to wait a while and see what's what."

Mike would be sitting in some bar, drinking, drinking. *Maybe, he'll call me. Maybe.*

The indefinable apprehension which had been growing within her began taking on shape and substance. She stood up, started pacing up and down her room. Suddenly she spun toward the telephone.

She called Ted's number. Then:

"Ted, you told him she'd be with Womack, didn't you? If Mike's been calling Eve at intervals and if she hasn't answered—"

She heard Ted's gasping oath.

"Sally, you've got something there. He'll be pouring grog into himself, wondering if there could be anything in the stuff he heard from me. He knows me. He'll finally realize I wasn't sounding off just to hear my own voice. God, he's liable to bust into Womack's and maybe he hasn't a gun, but he has a pair of murderous fists. He'll maim that little bastard and there'll be no extenuating circumstances so far as a jury's concerned. Eve's legally divorced from him." His voice trailed off, his words became incoherent.

"Ted. Keep your head! We've got to think of something to do."

"Hell, I can't think. But, maybe—yes, maybe if I could get Womack's phone number, call him, tell him to get Eve out of there... But I'd have to find someone from New World. The damned number is unlisted."

Level-headed Ted going to pieces at a time like this! Sally fought down her panic. "Ted, get in your car and come over for me. We're going out to Womack's. Maybe we can get there before Mike."

Mike walked out of the phone booth. Eve's number still didn't answer. He signaled for another drink and scowled down at his wristwatch. He closed one eye. Quarter past ten. Mighty long session with that coach. He gulped down his drink, remembering Ted's comment.

Dramatic coach. That's good. Womack will be coaching her, all right—in his bedroom.

What a foul, contemptible thing for Ted to say about the cleanest, purest girl in this rotten town. Mike flung down his glass with a curse. To make a crack like that about an unsophisticated girl who—

The bartender reached out and put a hand on his shoulder. " 'Bout time you laid off, fella. You've put away plenty."

Mike glowered at the blurred face on the other side of the bar. "Go away. I've got to think."

Something had been edging into his mind just as the bartender had spoken. What was it? Mike ran the back of his hand across his eyes. Whatever it was seemed to elude him.

Then it came to him: *An unsophisticated girl who'd kiss a man like Carrol Black, just to be friendly, would be naive enough to actually believe that an old debauchee like Womack had invited her to his home merely to help her with her lines.*

"Where's the nearest taxi stand?"

"Right up at the corner, fella."

Mike hurled himself out of the bar, ran to the end of the block. Gripping the cab driver's arm, he said hoarsely: "Know where Basil Womack lives?"

"Nope. Can't say as I got any idea."

"Listen, I've got to see him. He's a big-wheel producer."

The driver took off his cap and scratched his head. "Well, maybe we can get one of them maps they sell in drugstores and places. Shows where all these celebrities live."

Mike was out of the cab before it had come to a stop. "Wait here," he called out over his shoulder as he ran toward the wide entrance way.

His mouth felt cottony-dry; there was a choking sensation in his throat. If Womack had as much as touched her, he'd kill the vile little bastard.

He tried the door. It was locked. Too massive to shove in with a shoulder. His finger pressed the doorbell. Maybe he'd better bust in a window.

He was still pressing the doorbell when he saw the butler.

"Sir!" the man said with a pained expression on his face.

Mike grabbed the man's shoulder. "Listen to me. My wife's here with Womack. Where are they?"

"Nobody's here, sir. Nobody." Fear had brought a greenish tinge to the sallow face.

"Am I going to have to beat it out of you?" Mike's right hand lashed out. "Now talk, damn you, or—"

"Upstairs, the third door—"

He hurled the butler aside and ran up the stairs. All the doors.

He was blinded by the light, by the score of naked bodies, by the incredible, lewd orgy—beautiful white bodies and malformed hairy figures. Seconds passed before he realized that, in this mirrored room, there was only Womack—and Eve. Mike stood there, dazed. It was as if his brain refused to register this scene before his eyes.

And then, he retched.

Basil Womack cried out, startled: "What the hell!"

Eve looked up. A cry burst past her lips when she saw the grimace of rage that was distorting Mike's features. His lips were drawn back over his teeth: "Why, you slut! You unbelievable little slut! I'm going to kill you."

Womack cringed like a frightened animal, whimpering, "You can't blame me."

With a furious blow, Mike sent him reeling across the room. Eve backed off, looking about wildly for a way of escape. Mike went toward her with the measured step of an executioner.

She screamed, "Mike! Please! Mike!"

"There's a cab parked in front of Womack's." Ted slammed on the brakes.

They didn't pause to ask the driver if Mike had been his passenger. Somehow, they both knew. Ted ran ahead, began pounding on the door with one hand while he rang the bell with the other. Sally had reached his side when the butler, his face a grotesque mask of fright, opened the door and croaked:

"Something terrible's happening. Get help."

An agonized scream reached their ears. Ted flew up the stairs, Sally at his heels.

There was another tortured cry: "No, Mike!" And then, there was a blood-chilling silence.

Mike felt his fingers tighten about her throat. Tighter, tighter—He looked down into the reddening face, into the bulging eyes. No beauty there. Nothing but evil.

There was a roaring sound in his ears, a thunderous clamoring that deafened him. And there was a terrible strength in him, a maniac strength that foiled the efforts of those shadowy creatures who were trying to stop him from choking the life out of Eve. But, nothing could stop him now. Nothing—

"Mike! Stop it, Mike."

He heard it over the tumultuous din that resounded in his skull. His hands slipped away from Eve's throat.

Through a red mist, he looked down at the floor, at the limp body. Ted was kneeling at its side.

"He killed her, didn't he." The voice came from the hairy, gnome-like figure cowering in the corner. "Christ, a thing like this will ruin me."

Then, Ted's voice: "Sally, tell that ass of a butler to call a doctor. Eve's just out from shock. We made it here in time."

Mike put his arm over his eyes. Their voices were so quiet. Everything was so quiet, now. He turned and started from the room. Ted's voice reached him, softly, yet so distinctly:

"Let him go, Sally. You'll see him tomorrow. He'll come back to you. He always has—and he always will."

THE END